PILLOW KNOWS, THE TRUTH

Whispers in the Night, Secrets in the Stitch

Shalini V Samson

BlueRose ONE
Stories Matter
NewDelhi • London

BLUEROSE PUBLISHERS
India | U.K.

BlueRose ONE
Stories Matter
NewDelhi • London

For permissions requests or inquiries regarding this publication, please contact:

BLUEROSE PUBLISHERS
www.BlueRoseONE.com
info@bluerosepublishers.com
+91 8882 898 898
+4407342408967

ISBN: 978-93-7018-197-7

Cover design: Shubham Verma
Typesetting: Sagar

First Edition: May 2025

CONTENTS

Chapter 1

THE VOW

Soon, the newlyweds settled into a small cottage nestled near a tranquil lake. It was a picture-perfect beginning, a dream come true for Angel.

Time flew by. A year later, they welcomed their first son, Andrew Fernandez, named after father. Three years passed, and another son, Anthros Fernandez, joined their family. The townsfolk affectionately began referring to them as the "A" family, a testament to the unique bond they shared. Others simply called them the Fernandez's, a name that resonated with warmth and familiarity.

Life unfolded in a gentle rhythm. The boys grew, and Anthony, a skilled hunter, often took them on excursions into the nearby woods. Andrew, following in his father's footsteps, developed a passion for hunting. Anthros, however, found solace in the lake, fascinated by the smooth, colorful pebbles he collected.

One day, while engrossed in his search for the perfect pebble, Anthros heard the sharp crack of a gunshot. Fear gripped him, and he instinctively ducked behind a large oak tree. Peeking out cautiously, he witnessed a horrifying sight: Andrew, his face pale with shock, cradled a lifeless bear cub in his arms.

Anger surged through Anthros. "Andrew! How could you?" he yelled, his voice trembling with fury. A heated argument erupted between the brothers. Just as the situation threatened to escalate further, another gunshot echoed through the woods. Anthros, peering around the tree, saw his father standing over the slain mother bear. A chilling laugh escaped his father's lips.

Andrew, ignoring his father's grim expression, proudly displayed the cub on his shoulder. "Look, Papa!" he exclaimed.

Anthony's face hardened. "You should never kill a cub alone, son," he said sternly, his voice laced with disapproval. "Always kill the mother with it." He then turned to Anthros, his eyes twinkling with a mischievous glint. "And if you ever fight with your brother again," he warned, "you'll see the consequences."

He playfully tugged on Anthros' ears, much to the amusement of Andrew. The incident, though unsettling, soon faded into a distant memory as the brothers, hand in hand, walked back towards home, leaving the orphaned cub behind.

But Anthros could not shake off the image of the weeping cub beside its lifeless mother. He felt a pang of guilt, a profound sense of pity for the creature. He returned to the spot, his heart heavy. Gathering some discarded blankets and sheets from his room, he carefully constructed a small shelter for the cub, naming it Ash, after the greyish black fur that covered its tiny body.

An unlikely friendship blossomed between Anthros and Ash. While Andrew followed in his father's footsteps, taking over the family's wood and leather business, Anthros, inspired by his mother's gentle nature, pursued his dream of becoming a doctor. Ash, meanwhile, thrived in the dense forest, growing stronger each day.

Ash and Anthros raced into the forest laughing and enjoying themselves.

Despite their shared childhood, the brothers grew into vastly different men. Anthros, the epitome of his mother's nurturing spirit, remained his mothers' favorite. Andrew, mirroring his father's rugged individualism, often clashed with his mother. These differences inevitably led to frequent arguments, creating a rift within the family.

One night, after a particularly grueling night shift at the hospital, Anthros fell asleep, exhausted. Suddenly, a cacophony of sounds erupted. Andrew, fueled by anger, had stormed into Anthros' room, throwing his belongings around in a fit of rage.

Anthros, startled awake, confronted his brother. The argument escalated rapidly, voices rising in a heated exchange.

Angel, their mother, rushed in, her heart aching as she witnessed the escalating tension.

But her attempts to calm the situation proved futile. The fight spiraled out of control. In a moment of blind fury, Andrew, driven by a surge of anger, grabbed Anthros and dragged him towards the lake.

Suddenly, a terrifying roar shattered the night. A massive bear emerged from the dense undergrowth; its eyes gleaming with predatory intent. Terror gripped Andrew. He scrambled up the nearest tree, leaving Anthros alone to face the enraged beast.

The bear approached Anthros, its massive paws scraping against the ground. To Andrews' astonishment, the bear merely sniffed him curiously, then licked his face gently.

Just as the bear was about to turn away, a gunshot rang out. Angel, their mother, lay lifeless on the ground, a single bullet wound her chest.

Anthros let out a bloodcurdling scream. The bear, startled by the gunshot, retreated into the forest.

Andrew, scrambling down the tree, cried out, "Amma! Amma!"

But it was too late. Angel, her eyes glazed over, whispered something to Anthros before succumbing to her injuries.

Grief consumed Andrew, his cries echoing through the night. But Anthros was frozen in shock, his mind reeling.

Anthony came running towards hugged her still body and cried remembering the VOW

"I, Anthony Fernandez, take you, Angel Gabriel, to be my wife. Through every year, every minute, and every circumstance of my life, I will remain constant in my commitment towards you. I pledge this in the name of The Father, The Son, and The Holy Spirit."

Anthony, his face contorted with rage and grief, blamed Anthros for the tragedy. "You caused this!" he roared, his voice thick with anger. He lashed out at Anthros, the leather belt stinging his flesh.

Andrew, horrified by his father's violence, tried to intervene, but Anthony was beyond reason. Driven to the brink, Anthros, his mind clouded with rage and despair, fled from the scene, seeking solace in the sanctuary of the church.

Andrew hid himself behind the tree not to know what is to be done? Andrew saw Ash who was witnessing everything from far. He remembered how he separated his mother from him and cried with folded hands.

Time, though heals everything but has the power to repeat itself. Time: gives the deepest wound and leaves a scar.

Chapter 2

THE CHURCH

St. Francis Church, nestled in Vasco da Gama, Goa, was a beacon of hope, kept alive by the tireless efforts of Father Fernandez. The church buzzed with life, its walls echoing with the laughter of children from the adjoining orphanage. Among these children was Raghu Bhaiya, a thin Bengali man whose culinary skills nourished young hearts.

Raghu Bhaiya's life took an unexpected turn when he brought his cousin, Raghothri, to the orphanage. The children, ever quick with nicknames, affectionately dubbed him "Ragh Bhaiya" as well. Raghothri possessed a melodious voice that filled the orphanage with enchanting tunes.

Time marched on, and the leadership of the church shifted with the arrival and departure of various priests. Then came Father Fernandez, a man who profoundly impacted young Anthony. Impressed by Anthony's dedication and spirit, Father Fernandez became his mentor, a confidante in whom Anthony poured his heart. In gratitude, Anthony added "Fernandez" to his surname, a gesture that initially drew mixed reactions from his peers. Some mocked him, while others offered congratulations, ultimately embracing him with admiration. Even Raghu Bhaiya, known for his stern demeanor, softened his tone towards Anthony, recognizing the profound influence of Father Fernandez.

The tranquility of their lives was shattered by the news of a nine-year-old girl's abduction. The news sent shockwaves through Goa, casting a long shadow over the community. Though the initial wave of fear subsided, the missing girl, Swizel, remained a constant presence in Father Fernandez's prayers. Curious, Anthony inquired about Swizel, prompting the priest to reveal that he had visited the girl's home twice, a remote location. Intrigued, Anthony expressed a desire to visit the family, a request that Father Fernandez readily granted.

The following morning, Anthony eagerly prepared for the journey. Father Fernandez awaited him, and together they embarked on their journey at dawn. The cool morning air whipped against their faces as they rode, a sense of adventure stirring within Anthony. They paused at a roadside tea stall, where Father Fernandez shared his wisdom about the journey, imparting valuable life lessons.

After a short ride, they reached their destination. As they dismounted, a young girl named Angel, 15 years, stood near the gate, greeting Father Fernandez with a warm smile. Anthony was captivated by her beauty – her eyes shone with an ethereal light, her lips were a delicate rose, and a distinctive mark on her left cheek added a touch of uniqueness.

Angel resided in Agonda, her home a stilt house nestled amidst the beauty of the beach. Her father, Mr. Sebastian Gabriel, the beach caretaker, had meticulously maintained the surrounding area. Mr. Gabriel had two daughters: Angel and

Swizel, his step daughter. Though he loved both his daughters equally, the lingering shadow of the past often cast a pall over their lives. Ann Martin, Angels' mother, harbored resentment, believing that June Feroz had driven away her husband, and given them Swizel. The anger towards her husband was not receded yet.

Both girls were undeniably beautiful, each with their own distinct charm. Swizel, with her slender frame, blonde hair, and captivating eyes, possessed a delicate allure. Angel, however, exuded a captivating radiance.

Mr. Gabriel, a tall man with a slightly stooped posture, welcomed them warmly. He served them a simple meal of chapati and pork curry, his hospitality radiating warmth. As they conversed, Ann mentioned the agonizing six months since Swizel's disappearance, her voice tinged with sadness. Father Fernandez offered words of comfort, assuring her of his continued search.

Noticing Angel's interest in music, Father Fernandez suggested guitar lessons. Mr. Gabriel, initially hesitant about Angel venturing out alone, readily agreed when Father Fernandez offered to have Anthony accompany her.

Delighted by the prospect, Anthony eagerly anticipated their Wednesday and Friday lessons, the appointed days for Angel's guitar classes. Initially, their interactions were brief, limited to polite exchanges and shy smiles. However, Anthony found himself drawn to her, observing her intently as she played, her fingers dancing across the strings.

The church remained Anthony's sanctuary, but his life had taken on a new dimension. His friendship with Mr. Gabriel deepened, and his admiration for Angel blossomed with each passing day.

Chapter 3

FALLING IN LOVE

Years passed. Anthony and Angel had grown accustomed to each other's presence. One day, Angel abruptly announced to Father Fernandez that she no longer wished to learn guitar. When pressed for a reason, she remained silent and retreated home. Anthony's heart sank. He spent months walking past her house, stealing glances from afar.

One afternoon, Anthony witnessed a horrifying scene. Ragh Bhaiya was arguing aggressively with Angel and her mother. He grabbed Angel's left hand, and she cried out in pain. Fury surged through Anthony. He could not contain himself and rushed to intervene. Angel, fearing for her safety, darted inside the house.

Anthony, in a fit of rage, attacked Ragh Bhaiya, pummeling him mercilessly. Ragh lay crumpled on the ground, blood staining his clothes. Angel watched the scene unfold in horror from the window, screaming for someone to stop the fight. Villagers alerted the police, and a young boy raced to the beach house to inform Sébastien.

Separating the two men proved a difficult task. The police apprehended Ragh Bhaiya, who was bleeding profusely, and bundled him into a jeep. Anthony was also detained.

Father Fernandez arrived at the police station and secured Anthony's release. The journey back to the orphanage was shrouded in silence. Father Fernandez dropped Anthony off at the dormitory before heading to the hospital with Ragh Bhaiya.

Ragh Bhaiya's injuries were significant. He had five stitches on his forehead, a fractured and twisted right arm, two missing teeth, and a bruised leg. The sight of him in such a state evoked a pang of sympathy in Anthony, despite his anger.

Upon returning from the hospital, Father Fernandez, enraged by Anthony's actions, stormed into his room and began to reprimand him harshly. Father instructed Anthony to reflect on his behavior and locked him inside a storage room filled with donated items.

Anthony, overwhelmed with guilt and fear, broke down in tears. He punched the wall in frustration and eventually succumbed to sleep without food or water.

A voice startled him awake. Peering through the window, he saw Ragh Bhaiya returning from the hospital in a small van. Anthony retreated further into the room, his fear escalating.

As he stumbled backward, he tripped over a box, sending its contents scattering. Inside, he saw a pillow. He picked it up, surprised by its weight, and placed it back in the box.

Suddenly, a knock on the door startled him. It was Father Fernandez.

"What are you doing here?" Father Fernandez inquired.

"Ragh Bhaiya is back, Father," Anthony stammered, his voice trembling. "I'm scared."

"Come with me to the dining hall right now," Father Fernandez instructed calmly.

The dining hall served as a multipurpose space for prayer and meals. Three long tables with benches lined the room, with additional smaller tables in the center. Anthony followed Father Fernandez, his gaze drawn to Angel and her parents seated on the left side of the hall, opposite Ragh Bhaiya. Father Xavier, high priest with a long beard, gray hair, and a stern expression, stood beside them. He was a strong man who had assumed his position after his father's recommendation to the high priest, Father Alex. Father Xavier, though a diminutive stature, was serving as the high priest at that time. A good listener but short-tempered Father, children feared him and use to call 'SMALL HITLER.' All eyes were on Father as he got down from his car. All were expecting some fierce scene will be there. He has kept a tall muscled man as his helper. He always carries a cane with him. No one dared enough to ask anyone the secret of his cane. Anthony's heart lurched as he noticed bruises on Angel's leg and left hand. How had he missed these injuries? he wondered, stricken with concern.

Both sides presented their accounts of the incident while Father Xavier meticulously documented everything. He then turned to Angel, his voice gentle. "Angel, what would you like to say?"

Tears welled up in Angel's eyes. A heavy silence descended upon the room. Mr. Sébastien shifted nervously in his seat, his mind racing with worry. Anthony glared at Ragh Bhaiya with barely contained rage.

Finally, Angel spoke, her voice trembling. "Ragh Bhaiya hurts me a lot."

Before Anthony could react, Father Xavier boomed, his voice laced with anger, "Who did you tell about this, Angel? Why didn't you confide in Father Fernandez?"

"I already told Ragh Bhaiya to stop," Angel replied defiantly.

Father Xavier's face flushed with anger asked his guard to use his cane, 5 times. Ragh was already in pain and he got 5 more, Anthony was damn happy and his face shared a smile of content. Father Fernandez gestured to him to be serious.

In the heat of the moment, Father Xavier turned to Anthony and, mistakenly assuming the worst, said, "She's being hurted by Raghotham. Are you involved in this?"

"No!" Angel and Anthony both cried out in unison.

Ragh Bhaiya vehemently denied the accusations. "I didn't do anything!"

Exasperated, Father Xavier addressed Ragotham. "Pack your bags and leave immediately." He then turned to Mr. Sébastien. "What remedy do you seek?"

Ann, Angel's mother, interjected before Mr. Sébastien could speak. "The decision should be hers," she declared firmly. I already lost my younger one and she started sobbing.

Angel, surprising everyone in the room, spoke up. "I don't want to marry anyone," she said. "But I want the pillow. I saw a pillow of my Swizel.‘’

Confused silence filled the hall as everyone looked at Angel. Father Xavier exclaimed! Father Fernandez, ever the pragmatist, quickly interjected. "Perhaps it would be best for Angel to marry Anthony," he suggested. "He clearly cares for her deeply, as evidenced by his actions towards Ragh Bhaiya."

Father Xavier, seemingly eager to resolve the situation, mumbled in agreement. "Let it be so."

Angel's gaze darted towards Anthony. He met her eyes and spoke softly, following Father Fernandez's lead. "As Father said," he began, "but perhaps we could give her some time. She has been through a lot, and it's important to be feel prepared. I love her and I can wait."

Relief washed over Angel's face. "Let us fall in love together, "Anthony added sincerely.

Love should be unbiased, unforceful and it should grow with a healthy fight and immense care. In True Love, we should see Empathy rather than Sympathy, thought Father Fernandrz looking at Anthony.

A sense of respect towards Father Xavier was developed in Anthony and he told all the dormitory students about the usage of cane. Every time he explained the usage of cane on Ragh Bhaiya, he smiled and others enjoyed and laughed. The dorm boys were very happy and they got new helper instead of Raghothri.

Days turned into weeks, and with each passing interaction, Anthony felt a deeper connection with Angel. She blossomed into a mature young woman, and their friendship blossomed into something more. One day, Angel, to everyone's delight, agreed to marry Anthony.

The wedding ceremony was a simple affair, it went, held in a room provided by Father Fernandez. The newlyweds embarked on their married life together, filled with happiness and hope for the future.

After completing his Bachelor of Science degree in computer science, Anthony set out to find a job. He landed a modest position in finance at a local general store. Meanwhile, Angel reveled in her role as a homemaker, honing her culinary skills to Anthony's delight.

Their peaceful existence continued for a while. However, a new desire stirred within Anthony. He expressed his wish to move to Canacona, a beach area, seeking a change of scenery.

Initially apprehensive, Angel eventually came around to the idea. The move proved to be a turning point in their relationship. Living near the beach fostered a sense of closeness between them. Anthony's love for Angel deepened with each passing day, and their bond grew stronger as they built their life together.

Anthony, being exploring in nature, always likes to have a quick nature visit and he started hunting along with farming and they started their life journey. Anthony slowly put himself backward from the Sunday service and usually visits Father Fernandez on weekdays but Angel never missed a single day of Sunday Service. Father Fernandez knew everything about Anthony. Gradually Angel stated bringing her two boys to Sunday Service, imparting the idealism in them.

Everything is controlled by God and we are His potters, He plans the perfection in everything for us.

Chapter 4

FEAR

The insistent rapping on the church door startled Father Fernandez, a man whose hair had recently begun to silver

and whose eyes, now aided by spectacles, struggled to adjust to the dim light. With a hesitant gait, he approached the door, each latch clicking into place with a deliberate slowness. It was Anthros, his face a mask of grief, tears streaming down his cheeks.

Father Fernandez ushered him inside, his own heart heavy. He poured a glass of water, the trembling of his hands betraying his own inner turmoil. "Pa... Papa killed my mother," Anthros choked out, his voice raw with emotion.

Fear, cold and clammy, gripped Father Fernandez. He gently guided Anthros to a chair, his mind racing. How could he help this distraught child?

Raghu, the church caretaker, a man whose jovial demeanor was often overshadowed by a burgeoning belly, appeared in the doorway, his face a picture of concern. Father Fernandez, desperate to shield Anthros from further distress, shushed him with a finger to his lips.

Determined to act, Father Fernandez led Anthros to his private chambers, a small, dimly lit room affectionately called "Pillows" due to the soft cushions that lined its walls. He shades the door gently, a knot of anxiety tightening in his chest. He had to see Anthony, to understand.

The ride to Anthony's house was a blur. Images of Anthros' tear-stained face and the chilling accusation of murder haunted him. He returned to the church, his heart pounding. Anthros, thankfully, was sitting quietly in the prayer hall, his gaze fixed on a stained-glass window depicting the crucifixion. He had left Raghu in charge, a small comfort in the face of the growing unease.

At Anthony's house, the scene was chaotic. Anthony, his face contorted in grief, cradled Angel, his wife, in his arms. Andrew, his youngest, was nowhere to be found. The house was a wreck, overturned furniture and shattered glass testifying to a violent struggle.

Father Fernandez drew back to Anthony and offered Anthony a glass of water, his voice a gentle murmur. As Anthony recounted the events, his voice cracking with emotion, he remembered Andrew. "Angel... you must take care of Angel," he pleaded to Father, before rushing towards the lake, a desperate hope fueling his search.

Andrew, his eyes wide with terror, emerged from a thicket of bushes. "I don't want to see you," he stammered, his voice trembling. "You're a murderer! You took Mother away from us!"

Anthony's anguished cries echoed across the lake. "I was protecting you, Andrew! From Anthros! And from that bear."

Why are you always protecting us?

Angel, startled by the commotion, whimpered and tried to intervene. But the huge damage was done.

Father Fernandez, seeing Angel lying on the floor, called and informed police.

The arrival of the police, their faces grim, shattered the fragile calm. Andrew, overwhelmed by fear and guilt, confessed. The police, after a cursory examination, confirmed the worst: Angel lay lifeless on the floor, a victim of a tragic accident.

Anthony and Andrew were taken into custody, the image of Angel, still and lifeless, haunting them. Father Fernandez, his heart heavy with grief and disbelief, followed them in his bike, the weight of the tragedy pressing down on him.

On the way Anthony remembered the smile they shared and the love they had towards each other. Andrew was sobbing a lot thinking how much he argued with his mother and still she took the bullet for them.

It is always like that when the pain scorches it moves the deepest of deepest cells making the heart heavy and words to be silent.

Anthros was crying thinking his best friend, his only listener, was gone. He was crying in front of Jesus' cross.

Father Fernandez's heart was dropping and was thinking of Mr. Sebastien as he lost both the girls. He was thinking of Angel, how beautiful she was and how jovial girl she was, though she had a lot of issues regarding Anthony's habit but still she loved him like her own.

We always remember the words of old "value of eyes is only understood when we stop seeing" but it is not like that, people stop seeing from very early it is only understood when it is completely gone.

Anthony had immense love for Angel, but the power of money and hunting made Angel invisible. When that beautiful soul departed, he understood that he had already stopped noticing her.

Father Fernandez stopped in between and cried out loud.

All reached the police station. All were questioned and on the request of Father Fernandez, Police kept Anthony to their custody and Andrew was left. Father Fernandez and Andrew drew back.

Chapter 5

THE DARK ROOM

Panic seized Anthros as he fled his home from the church, the stench of decay clinging to him. He reached the tree house, his sanctuary, a refuge now transformed into a chamber of horrors. The smell, a sickening blend of rot and something metallic, assaulted his senses. He pushed open the door to Andrew's room, and the sight that met him nearly shattered his sanity.

Blood, dried and dark, stained the sheets, and a chillingly familiar object lay discarded nearby – the head of a man, the eyes gouged out. Anthros stumbled back, retching violently, the image seared into his memory.

Then, a chilling whisper echoed in his mind – his mother's desperate plea, "P...illows." He scrambled back to his room, grabbing a handful of the stones he had collected over the years, a desperate act of self-preservation. He fled the scene, leaving the tree-house open, the horrors within a testament to unimaginable evil.

Meanwhile, Inspector Khan Mathews, a man of steely resolve and a troubled past, with pointy nose and good sense of humor always carried a packet of chewing gum with him, was investigating the disappearance of Anthros from the church. He took Andrew from the church with the permission of Father Fernandez. Inspector Khan was a psychologist turned detective, driven by a relentless pursuit of truth. As he gathered information, Daya, a concerned neighbor, informed him of Anthros' arrival. Just now he left towards the woods, police ran and caught him, inspector Khan stayed there only. When Anthros was bought back, Inspector Khan

"Don't you want to meet your father?" Inspector Khan inquired; his voice sharp.

Anthros, however, only demanded to see Andrew.

Ignoring protocol, Inspector Khan allowed the meeting, sensing a unique opportunity to unlock the truth. The brothers faced each other, an eerie silence hanging in the air. Then, Andrew, overcome with grief and guilt, broke down. For the first time in their lives, they embraced a fragile bond forged in the face of unspeakable tragedy.

"Why did you fight with me?" Anthros whispered, his voice trembling.

Andrew, his gaze darting around the room, confessed, "In the tree house, there was something... I thought you did it, to trap me."

Before Andrew could elaborate, Inspector Khan intervened, "Separate them," he ordered. "Prepare a vehicle. We're going to the tree house."

Andrew and Anthros exchanged terrified glances. Inspector Khan, his eyes gleaming with a chilling intensity, revealed, "You didn't see the screw camera installed under the table."

The brothers, their faces pale, were led to the tree house. Father Fernandez, the local priest, was summoned to provide background on the 'Mr. A' family. As they examined the scene, a horrifying discovery awaited them – the head found earlier, confirming their worst fears.

The forensics team, along with search dogs, descended upon the scene. Hours into the search, Inspector Khan, weary and frustrated, lit a cigarette. "Father Fernandez," he said, "tell me everything you know about this family."

Father Fernandez, his voice heavy with sorrow, recounted the tragic history of Anthony, Angel, and Raghothri, their former cook at the orphanage.

"Who is this man?" Inspector Khan pressed, referring to the head.

"Raghothri," Father Fernandez replied, I saw him after many years and that too this way, his voice barely a whisper.

Inspector Khan remained unconvinced but continued to gather information. Suddenly, a chilling cry pierced the air, "Sir, look at this!"

It was the body, or rather, half of it. Disbelief washed over the investigators. The stench emanating from the head was overpowering. The forensics team meticulously collected the remains. Inspector Khan, his stomach churning, retched violently. As he washed his face, he looked at the body, he felt like its Mary's feet but he turned and murmured NO, My Mary is still alive.

"There must be more," he declared, his voice grim.

The search resumed, and soon, a gruesome discovery was made – the lower extremities of the body, lying a short distance away. The news spread like wildfire, attracting a swarm of reporters. The case, initially intended for utmost confidentiality, was now splashed across headlines, causing a media frenzy.

Panicked by the intense media scrutiny and pressure from higher authorities, Inspector Khan returned to the police station and summoned Anthony for interrogation. He slapped the man repeatedly, his anger boiling over.

"What is this?" Khan demanded, brandishing the gruesome photographs he had taken. "Tell me the truth, or I'll make you talk!"

Anthony, instead of breaking down, erupted in a chilling laughter. Inspector Khan, enraged, lashed out with his belt. But Anthony continued to laugh, a chilling, unnerving sound.

Then, a message arrived from Inspector Rekha from the forensics lab. "Sir, you need to see this."

Khan rushed to the forensic lab, where the body lay arranged – head, upper torso, and then, separately, the lower extremities.

"Why are they separated?" Khan demanded.

"They don't match," Rekha replied, her voice somber. "There are two bodies. We have one half, the upper half of this body is missing and the lower half of the other one."

Khan was stunned.

"And," Rekha continued, "the other body is female, possibly a minor. She has been subjected to repeated assault. And look here, on her left thigh…"

She pointed to a chilling detail, "It's carved… 'Pillows.'

Inspector Abhishek, his face pale, asked, "How can you be sure?"

"It's carved deep," Rekha confirmed, " See, it's visible clearly."

The truth, more horrifying than anyone could have imagined, was slowly emerging from the shadows.

Khan was devastated as some of the memories of his sister flushed into his brain, he rushed out and vomited.

Chapter 6
PILLOWS

Inspector Khan and Abhishek began their interrogation with Andrew, who claimed ignorance. "I don't know anything, Sir," he stated. "I started beating Anthros when I saw a head in my treehouse. I always go hunting. My father has a licensed gun given by Father Xavier. He's very friendly and always used to stay in the treehouse."

Inspector Khan instructed Abhishek to summon Father Xavier and call him. Interrupting the interrogation with Andrew, Khan examined Anthros' room, finding some correlation between his and Andrew's statements. However, Anthros exhibited noticeable unease upon hearing about the second body being female, despite denying any knowledge of the bodies.

Father Xavier arrived, and Khan, ignoring phone calls, greeted him. "Good afternoon, Father," Khan said.

Father Xavier sat on a low chair, and Khan promptly ordered cushions for his comfort. "I can definitely say that you are questioning the wrong person," Father Xavier declared.

"I didn't ask any questions," Khan replied. "Now I am going to ask, Sir. Please tell me, did you give licensed guns to Anthony?"

"Yes," Father Xavier replied.

"How many guns do you have?"

"Three," the Father replied. "I keep them for show, I don't use them, out of which I gave one to Anthony."

"Oh! We have found two bodies from Anthony's house. You might have seen the news. Do you know anything about this?"

"No," Father Xavier replied firmly. "Who ordained you? That is none of your business. We have a higher priest who ordains us."

Khan dismissed Father Xavier, instructing Abhishek to escort him home. However, before he left, Khan asked, "Are you the son of Michael Xavier?"

"Yes," Father Xavier replied.

Khan was visibly shocked. A flashback surfaced: Michael Xavier, Xavi Anna (brother), and the tattoo of a lion face on his right wrist.

Khan sat for a moment, his mind racing with the flashback and the chilling screams of the girls.

Determined to uncover the truth, he instructed Abhishek to discreetly observe Father Xavier. Abhishek agreed, adding that no one spoke to him like that and that he had considerable influence in the area. Khan sensed a deeper concern in Abhishek's words and left the room, stepping outside for a cigarette.

Father Xavier returned home and contacted higher officials. Khan's phone rang incessantly, but he remained silent, his mind elsewhere. Abhishek called, "Sir, Anthros is calling... he wants to convey something." Khan immediately followed Abhishek. He instructed him to wait outside and entered the room where Anthros sat in a corner. Khan sat beside him.

"Everything changed, Khan," Anthros confessed. "I cannot find Ash anywhere. It was all your suggestion, but now it's turned upside down. I lost my mother after heeding your words."

Khan replied, "Everything is under control, Doctor ji. I am here. We found a half-body of a girl, and we have sent it for forensic examination. I hope this might not be my sister."

How come it is in the treehouse, did you question Father Xavier, my father is trapping me into this Khan. You know the whole story of my family. Whose skull was it? Oh…it was of Raghothri, a former cook in the orphanage confirmed by Father Fernandez. Anthros hugged Khan and cried a lot. My Amma….

Khan and Anthony were thick friends and they always shared a bond of being neglected by their fathers. Recently they met in the same hospital where Anthros was working as Khan was questioning a case of drugs.

"I saw Father Xavier today," Anthros continued. "Who was that person whose skull you have given me to keep in Andrew's room? I kept it and lost my mother. I should not have listened to you. You were my only best friend."

Khan replied, "I told you everything is under my control. I told you know, skull was of Raghothri,as I told you earlier, I found it while I was investigating the case of drugs. Do not worry. I will bring you out of this."

"Leave that matter," Khan insisted.

"I wanted to tell you that after seeing you, I ran and entered the church. Father Fernandez kept me in a room called 'Pillows.' I wanted to check it, but suddenly heard a knock. It was Father Fernandez himself as he returned halfway. He dragged me out of it and locked it and left." said Anthros.

Khan inquired, "Is there any room named or labeled like this?"

"No, I didn't see anyone," Anthros replied.

Khan left, instructing Abhishek to keep an eye on Anthros, fearing he might attempt suicide.

Khan retrieved the bullet by which Angel was murdered, and proceeded to the dormitory, where he inquired about Anthony. He summoned Raghu, Father Fernandez, and some of the workers.

Father Fernandez stated, "I already told you whatever I knew about them." Khan asked, "Can I visit your dormitory from outside? Can we walk?"

"Okay," Father Fernandez agreed.

As they walked, Khan inquired about Anthony's friends.

"Oh, not much," Father Fernandez replied. "He was very submissive and introverted. It was Father Xavier who started teaching him a lot. One day, there was no water in the dormitory, and all the children were complaining and misbehaving. He was the only one who drew water and encouraged all the children. From that day onwards, he became my favorite, and here all were making fun of me, saying, 'Anthony is your son.'" He laughed.

Khan purposefully stopped near the room labeled "Pillows," asking, "None of your rooms are labeled. How come this one is?"

"Oh, that's simple. We are renovating and going to label more rooms like this. I will show you," Father Fernandez replied. He asked Raghu to bring the key. Raghu returned with the key, and Khan opened the door.

It was a green-painted room with a red paint bathroom. Khan sensed something amiss. The explanation did not align with Anthros' statement. He realized he needed a search warrant.

Suddenly, Khan noticed Raghu's uneasy demeanor. He instructed Father Fernandez to send Raghu inside. "This room is best for interrogation," he said.

Father Fernandez complied. Khan made Raghu sit on a chair within the room.

"When was this room painted?" Khan asked.

Raghu replied, "Two days before... no, no, 10 days before."

"What was in this room?"

"Too many pillows," Raghu replied. "Some pillows were heavy, some were light, and names were engraved on them."

"Why were the names written, and whose names were they?"

"They were the names of all the girls who come for Sunday school and guitar practice," Raghu explained. "Classes are taken by Father Xavier. There were nearly twenty pillows."

"Now where are those pillows, and why did he keep their names as pillows?"

"Pillows?" Raghu stammered. "Father Xavier took them with him. On the completion of the guitar course, he used to give named pillows as their remembrance. He used to make a bag of remembrance."

"Have you seen any girl getting hurt during the class or anything?"

"Yes, yes," Raghu replied. "One girl named Mary, she might be of 13 or 14 years old. Khan turned, one day I saw her crying as Father Xavier scolded her for not concentrating in the class. Father took her inside this room, and after 5 minutes, she was alright."

"What makes you remember her name so well out of all the girls?"

"Oh, she was an angel," Raghu exclaimed. "Her lips were rose in color. I do not know about her parents, but her mother was converted. She was a Keralite as she spoke some of that kind of language in between. She was extremely beautiful, and so was her daughter, but her daughter was more beautiful. She was tall, fair, and intelligent. I have seen many girls as tourists and in this Sunday school, but no one was like her."

There was a knock at the door. Father Fernandez stood there with a cup of tea. Khan replied, "Some other day," and left.

Khan was deeply hurt and was thinking of his family. On his way back he met his mother in the asylum and memories surfaced, a small family. A family of four, Amma and Appa, Khan, and Mary. Mary being very naughty and mischievous, her laugh itself made us cherished, suddenly went missing and today is the fifteenth day.

Appa started drinking and amma showing the gestures of suicide. Khan was devastated and appealed not to share this to anyone and he will search silently. He reached his room and cleaned the whole area and cooked food for his father and himself. After doing the chores, he went into his room and saw Appa checking the notice board and they both searching for their Mary.

Chapter 7

THE TRUTH

The stench of sweat and fear hung heavy in the air as Khan returned to the police station, a bag of steaming hot lunch clutched in his hand. Anthony, his eyes sunken and his face pale, sat hunched over, the remnants of the pork curry scattered across the table.

"Here," Khan said, pushing the bag towards him. "Eat."

Anthony, ravenous, devoured the food with surprising ferocity. As he reached for the last chapati, a flicker of unease crossed his face.

He placed the bullet on the table 'This was the bullet we got from Angel's body.' Anthony sobbed loudly I will answer all your questions. Khan asked Pillows....

"Khan," he mumbled, his voice thick with the remnants of the meal, "Father Xavier... he had a pillow for every Sunday school student."

Khan's brow furrowed. "Every single one?"

"Yes," Anthony confirmed, chewing thoughtfully. "He said it was for remembrance. You know, like a keepsake."

"Remembrance?" Khan echoed, a chilling thought taking root in his mind. "What happened to these children that they needed to be remembered?"

Anthony shrugged, stuffing the last piece of chapati into his mouth. "Girls, Khan. That was the orphanage's policy. We had only boys."

Khan's gaze sharpened. "Then why the pillows?"

"Oh, the girls... they came for Sunday school," Anthony explained, "and for guitar lessons. Father Xavier would teach them himself. He couldn't carry the big guitar, you see, being... well, you know." He gestured vaguely towards his own diminutive stature. "So, he had his own, a beautiful one, in his room."

Anthony paused, his eyes darting nervously around the room. "I want water," he pleaded, his voice cracking.

Khan turned to Abhishek. "No water."

Panic seized Anthony. He began to tremble, his breathing ragged. "Please, Khan, I need water!"

Khan remained impassive. "The poison is taking effect."

Anthony's pleas grew desperate, but Khan turned away, his gaze fixed on the floor. Abhishek watched Anthony with a mixture of apprehension and morbid curiosity. The man's suffering was a spectacle, a twisted form of entertainment.

Finally, Khan relented. "Water," he barked at Abhishek. "But only one glass."

Abhishek, with a smirk, brought Anthony a glass of water. As the cool liquid touched his parched tongue, Anthony's eyes widened. A searing pain erupted in his throat, and he let out a strangled cry.

"Hospital!" Abhishek exclaimed, feigning alarm. "We need to get him to the hospital!"

Khan ignored him. "Anthony," he said, his voice low and menacing, "do you remember Mary K. Mathews?"

Anthony, gasping for breath, shook his head. "Mary? No, I don't remember her."

"Swizel?" Khan pressed.

"Yes, Swizel," Anthony whispered, his voice hoarse. "She was my Angels' younger sister." Anthony's voice breaking.

"How did she die?" Khan inquired; his eyes boring into Anthony's.

Anthony, his body wracked with convulsions, croaked, "I want water... more water..."

Khan gestured towards the glass. "Drink."

Anthony gulped down the remaining water, but the relief was fleeting. The burning sensation intensified, and he began to scream.

"We need to get him to a hospital!" Abhishek repeated, his voice laced with feigned urgency.

Khan ignored him. He pulled out a strip of Avil tablets. "This is all you get," he said, "if you tell me the truth."

Anthony's screams subsided into a series of desperate gasps. "The pillows," he wheezed, "they're in the basement. Father Xavier has the keys... with his car keys. And... there is a book... in Andrew's treehouse... it tells you everything..."

Anthony slumped back against the chair, unconscious. Abhishek, with a practiced air, caught him before he could fall. "0ne-Zero-Eight," he instructed, then turned to Khan. "I'll go with you, Sir. I'll help."

Khan hesitated, then nodded. "But you don't say a word to Father Xavier."

"Of course not, Sir," Abhishek assured him, his eyes gleaming with a predatory light. "You can trust me."

They hurried out of the station, leaving Anthony in the care of a bewildered Robin. As they drove towards the orphanage, Khan revealed his plan to Abhishek.

"We're going to get the diary first after we go to the basement," he said, his voice grim. "Then, we'll alert the forensics team."

Abhishek nodded eagerly. He was enjoying this far too much.

Reaching the tree-house, they found the grounds eerily silent. The swing set swayed gently in the breeze, a lonely sentinel in the fading light. They climbed the ladder to Andrew's treehouse, the air thick with the scent of old wood and dust.

Abhishek, his eyes darting around the room, let out a low whistle. "Sir, look at this!"

Scattered amongst Andrew's toys were a collection of intricately embroidered pillows, each bearing the name of a young-missing- girls. And on the bedside table, nestled amongst a pile of books, lay a leather-bound diary.

Abhishek picked up the diary, his fingers tracing the embossed initials: "R.V."

He opened it to the first page and gasped.

"Dear Khan," the entry began, "You are a smart police officer. I did not know you were Mary's brother. She was beautiful, pure as snow. When I touched her..."

Abhishek's voice trailed off, his eyes widening in horror. He looked up at Khan, his face pale. "Sir, this is... this is beyond anything I could have imagined."

Khan, his face etched with grief and fury, reached for the diary. But Rekha, the forensic expert, stepped forward.

"Sir," she said gently, "let us handle this."

Khan looked at her, his eyes brimming with tears. "Can you... can you open the first pillow labelled as Mary, Rekha?" he pleaded. "Please?"

Rekha, understanding the depth of his pain, nodded solemnly. As she carefully unzipped the pillow, a single, crimson rose petal fluttered to the ground, landing at Khan's feet.

The letter, stained with age, lay nestled amongst the stuffing. Khan reached for it, his fingers trembling.

"This game," the letter continued, "brings me passion for the dark world."

Yours,

R.V.

The weight of the revelation crashed down on Khan, leaving him reeling. The orphanage, a place of sanctuary and innocence, had become a chamber of horrors. And at the heart of it all was Father Xavier, the man who had been entrusted with the care of children.

Rekha commenced the task, her focus momentarily disrupted by her ringing phone. It was her mother.

"Amma, I'll be home in two days," she said, her voice strained.

"Alright, my dear," her mother replied, her voice brimming with pride, "You looked absolutely radiant on television. Don't forget to bring some coriander leaves."

Khan, his grief momentarily forgotten, watched as Rekha carefully opened Mary's pillow. A fragrant aroma, a peculiar blend of lavender and roses, wafted through the air. Inside, instead of feathers, lay a collection of smooth, round pebbles.

Each pebble, upon closer inspection, bore a single letter, forming a cryptic puzzle. Rekha, bewildered by this macabre discovery, immediately called for assistance. Two of her colleagues rushed to her aid.

The pebbles, each a unique shade of grey, had been arranged in a complex pattern, a cipher that had defied their initial attempts at decryption. They had tried every known method, from simple substitution to complex fractal analysis, yet the message remained stubbornly obscured. It was only when Lena noticed the subtle variations in the texture of the stones, the almost imperceptible etchings that formed a micro-script, that the puzzle began to unravel.

The final phrase, painstakingly pieced together from the micro-script and the spatial arrangement of the stones, hung in the air like a death knell:

"You should not laugh."

The words were stark, chilling, a stark contrast to the seemingly innocent, almost childlike, addition:

"Rosy lips

Dimple chin

Bubbly cheeks

Smiling within"

The juxtaposition was unsettling. The description, seemingly a playful poem, was now a source of dread. The "rosy lips" were no longer a symbol of innocent joy, but a potential mask, a deceptive facade. The "dimple chin," the "bubbly cheeks," the "smiling within" – all of them now carried a sinister undertone, a hidden sin carried with the girl.

Abhishek, his voice a low rasp, nodded slowly. "But why? Who would want to suppress laughter, to extinguish joy?" He ran a hand over his tired face. "And what does the description mean? Is it a person? A place? A symbol?"

The pebbles, once simply a puzzle, were now a harbinger of dread, a silent testament to a darkness lurking just beneath the surface.

See it has a letter too…..

A Letter

Dear XV

Take this pillow and keep it safe, this was my favorite. I need to make one more.

Yours RV

The room, once filled with the hushed whispers of conspiracy, now hung heavy with the weight of a chilling revelation. Twenty pillows, each a stark white canvas bearing the same unsettling message, lay scattered across the floor. The air crackled with a tension that could be cut with a knife.

Khan, his face a mask of grim determination, stood outside the window, the flickering orange glow of his cigarette a stark contrast to the pale moonlight. Each drag brought a deep inhale, the smoke swirling around him like a ghostly shroud.

Abhishek, ever the concerned friend, appeared with a steaming cup of tea, the aroma of cardamom and ginger a faint counterpoint to the suffocating atmosphere within.

"Who is Mary?" Abhishek's voice, though gentle, carried a tremor of unease.

Khan, finally extinguishing his cigarette, turned to face his friend. "She's my only sister," he began, his voice hoarse. Now she has become 'was.'

God gifted us after 16 years " Recently, she vanished. Poof! Gone without a trace."

The memory, a gaping wound in his past, seemed to momentarily overwhelm him. He took a deep breath, steadying himself. "I was searching for her. Everywhere. He paused, his gaze drawn to the pillows scattered across the floor. "Then, ten days ago, I heard that name again. From Father Fernandez. He… he knew something."

The unspoken words hung heavy in the air: Father Fernandez spoke of her name. I could not ask him in detail. What connection did Mary have to this gruesome mystery? And what did the reappearance of her name of silence truly signify?

Who is RV now? asked Abhishek, suddenly.

Did you check the letter? There are two people.

I think Father Xavier has personality disorder, he is making fun of ours, doing this crap and making us running here and there. Let's question him in detail.

Sir, this letter is written with ink mixed with blood. It matches with Mary's and one thing the lower extremites of the body which we found from the Andrew's treehouse matches with Mary. It is Mary's half. Rekha said pointing towards the body, hearing this Khan fainted and ended up in hospital with Abhishek.

Upon gaining conscious Khan said ' we need to grab Anthony'.

Abhishek said ' What if Andrew knew something?'

Rekha knocked at the door saying' Sorry Sir, I revealed the news in this way. That's ok. He turned and asked Abhishek 'Be ready with the jeep, I am coming. They left.

Chapter 8

THE IDENTITY

The humid Goan air hung heavy, the sky a canvas of bruised purple and bruised orange. Abhishek and Inspector Khan stood on the balcony of the police station, the city lights twinkling below like a distant constellation. A silence, heavy with unspoken anxieties, stretched between them.

"Sir," Robert's voice broke through the stillness, "You should see this."

They hurried down to the forensic laboratory, the air thick with the metallic tang of chemicals. Rekha, the forensic scientist, gestured towards a table where two halves of a human torso lay side-by-side.

"Look," she said, her voice hushed, "This is the other half of Mary, which we got from under tree- house. The other half of the body is this PILLOW. The DNA match is perfect."

Rekha took hold of Khan's hand saying "Khan, I understand what this letter means, written by the killer 'I need to make one more'. The other half of the body was still to be turned into pebbles.... Its 'BONE PEBBLES'

Khan cried loudly…..

A chilling realization dawned on Inspector Khan. "Anthony," he breathed, his eyes narrowing. His treehouse, my dear Mary, Khan broke the glass table.

He stormed out of the lab, his mind a whirlwind of suspicion and dread. He burst into Anthony's room, the air thick with the scent of expensive cologne and the faint aroma of old books. He said I want to go home and pray for Angel.

''Anthony'' inspector Khan said, all evidence is against you.

Oh, now what you found against me? I did not want to kill Angel; I was protecting her from the bear.

"Anthony," Inspector Khan demanded, his voice low and dangerous, "Where were you the night Mary disappeared?"

Anthony, ever the suave charmer, feigned innocence. "Inspector, I don't know Mary."

Inspector Khan did not buy it. He knew Anthony, knew his connection with Father Xavier and Father Fernandez.

Anthony, his smile faltering, reached for a nearby glass of water and hurled it across the room.

Inspector Khan remained unconvinced. He left Anthony's room, the unsettling image of the two halves of Mary's body seared into his memory.

Back at the cell, Anthros sat brooding, the weight of the discovery pressing down on him. He missed the jungle, the symphony of sounds, the vibrant hues of the rainforest. He longed for the companionship of his bear, a creature of gentle wisdom and unwavering loyalty.

Khan asked you are the one who collected Pebbles....did you collect Bone pebbles.....Anthros not answering,

"Ash," he whispered, a wistful smile gracing his lips. "I wonder what you're doing right now."

He imagined his bear, perhaps perched on a moss-covered rock, surveying the jungle with its keen eyes, the sunlight filtering through the leaves, dappling its fur in patches of gold. He yearned to be with him, to share his burdens, to find solace in the bear's quiet strength.

Inspector Khan, his face grim, entered the room. "Anthros" he said, "I need your help. We're taking Father Xavier into custody."

Anthros nodded, his thoughts still with his bear. He knew he had to focus, to help bring the killer to justice. But a part of him ached for the tranquility of the jungle, for the unconditional love of his bear.

As they prepared to leave the station, a strange sensation washed over Anthros. A tingling sensation, as if a distant voice were calling to him. He froze, his eyes widening.

"Inspector," he stammered, "Stop! I... I can hear him."

Inspector Khan, confused, stopped abruptly. "Hear who, Anthros?"

Anthros shook his head, a look of terror creeping into his eyes. "Ash. My bear. He's calling me."

Inspector Khan exchanged a bewildered glance with Abhishek. Anthros, usually so composed, was clearly unraveling.

"What do you mean, you can hear him?" Inspector Khan pressed; his voice laced with suspicion.

Anthos, his voice trembling, whispered, "He's in danger. I... I can feel it."

Inspector Khan, intrigued. "Where is he?"

Anthros, his eyes wide with a mixture of fear and longing, pointed towards the dense jungle that shrouded the outskirts of the city. "Deep within. I must go to him. I need to protect him."

Abhishek, his heart pounding, felt a strange sense of foreboding. Anthros' words, though seemingly delusional, resonated with a deep truth within him. He knew, with a certainty that defied logic, that bear was in danger. And somehow, Anthros, despite his flaws, was the only one who could help.

Inspector Khan, after a moment of hesitation, granted Anthros permission to go. He could not explain the inexplicable, but something in demeanor, the raw fear and desperate urgency in his eyes, convinced him that this was no mere act of defiance.

As Anthros rushed towards the jungle, a sense of unease settled over Abhishek. He knew, with a chilling certainty, that this was not just a rescue mission. This was a journey into the heart of darkness, a descent into the abyss of Angel's twisted soul.

And somewhere deep within the emerald labyrinth of the jungle, his bear waited, unaware of the impending danger, his gentle spirit oblivious to the storm that was about to break.

With permission. Abhishek followed Anthros into the dense forest, just to know the truth. He saw Anthros playing with the bear and cubs,

oh boy! You became a father, suddenly a gunshot, Abhishek interrupted. It was Silas with his friends in a jeep wanted to hunt the bear. Anthros came in between and a bullet pierced his leg, resulting in the bear growing wild. Ash followed Silas and, in a jump, pulled him out of the jeep only to devour him but Abhishek called ASH, LEAVE HIM. BEAR LEFT HIM.

Abhishek caught hold of Silas and his gang, and took Anthos to a nearby hospital in the same jeep. Anthros in pain told Silas, how many lives will you take more?

Chapter 9:

ANGEL'S BURIAL

The freshly dug grave was like a wound, matching the one in my heart. The heavy rain blurred my vision as I watched Angel's shiny wooden coffin being lowered into the ground. It was so different from the lively person she was. Father Fernandez thought how a single bullet had ended her life.

The air smelled of wet earth and lilies, a sad, heavy scent. People in black umbrellas stood together, their faces full of sadness. Whispers of sympathy and shock filled the air.

Anthony stood alone, his face showing deep guilt. His easy, privileged life was now full of pain and regret. The gun he used for sport had taken the life of the woman he loved.

I remembered Angel's bright smile and her dreams for the future. Those dreams were now buried with her. It was a cruel twist that the love she valued had caused her death. The saying "you reap what you sow" felt painfully true. Anthony's careless action had led to this terrible loss.

Anthros and Andrew, who used to be so cheerful, looked like shadows of themselves. Their faces were pale and sad, reflecting our shared grief. Our friendship felt fragile, broken by sorrow.

Father Xavier said the final prayers, but the words offered little comfort. Every shovelful of dirt hitting the coffin felt like a blow to my heart. The sound of crying rose and fell with the rain, a sad song for a life that ended too soon.

As the sun set and long shadows fell across the cemetery, Anthros stayed by the grave, unable to leave. The world felt cold and empty without Angel's warmth. The rain kept falling, washing away tears but not the pain. All that was left was the memory of her, bright and alive. It felt so unfair, like the world had turned upside down. Andrew saw Anthros's pain, not just for Angel, but for the broken pieces of their life. Now they are scared of Anthony.

Anthony was taken back to his cell, and Anthros and Andrew went to Angel's house. Anthros hugged Andrew and cried deeply.

"Life is like that," Khan thought to himself. "Sadness makes life even sadder. No matter what we do, life has its own way. Some call it 'karma,' but I call it God's lessons." Thought Fernandez. The people who have pride in anything at last, that particular thing itself becomes a noose for the neck.

Anthros and Andrew were relieved as they didn't carry any evidence to hold on but upon instruction by Khan to summon them while questioning..... Father Fernadez arranged everything for the boys. In their house itself.

Chapter 10

THE SHADOW OF DOUBT

Father Xavier was taken into custody by the higher authorities for interrogation. One whole night he was kept inside the cell. He hung himself in the cell.

The news of Father Xavier's death sent shockwaves through the tranquil Goan village. The revered priest, known for his kindness and compassion, had been found hanging in his cell, a suicide note scrawled on a piece of paper:

"I take all the charge."

"XV."

The villagers were inconsolable, struggling to comprehend the loss of their beloved spiritual guide.

Inspector Khan, a seasoned officer from the mainland, was burdened to investigate the case. The initial findings were puzzling. The post-mortem revealed that Father Xavier had not committed suicide; he had been murdered. The neatly tied noose, the position of the body, and the lack of any signs of a struggle pointed to a deliberate act, a cold-blooded killing.

The police station, despite being under constant surveillance, offered no clues. The CCTV footage, reviewed meticulously, showed no unauthorized entry or exit. The guards on duty swore they had not seen or heard anything unusual that night. The investigation hit a dead end.

The village, once a haven of peace, was now shrouded in fear and suspicion. Whispers and rumors spread like wildfire, each more unsettling than the last. Villagers, once united in their grief, now eyed each other with apprehension. The shadow of doubt fell upon everyone, casting a pall of gloom over the community.

Inspector Khan, a man of logic and reason, found himself grappling with a mystery that defied explanation. The lack of evidence, the absence of any clear motive, and the chillingly efficient manner of the murder left him baffled. He spent countless hours poring over the case files, interviewing villagers, and scrutinizing every detail, searching for any anomaly, any piece of information that might unlock the puzzle.

He interviewed Anthony and two boys, seeking any clues about his relationship in death with Father Xavier. They spoke of a strained relationship, a growing resentment between the young man and the priest. Anthony, a rebellious soul, had often clashed with Father Xavier's conservative views, leading to heated arguments. He was his father figure, gave him a gun and all expensive gifts. However, no concrete evidence linked Anthony to the murder.

Khan also delved into Father Xavier's past, hoping to uncover any hidden enemies, any unresolved conflicts that might have led to his demise. He discovered that the priest had once been embroiled in a land dispute with a neighboring village, a conflict that had escalated into bitter animosity. However, years had passed since then, and the feud seemed to have subsided.

As the investigation dragged on, the pressure mounted on Inspector Khan. The villagers, desperate for answers, grew increasingly impatient with the lack of progress. The media, sensing a sensational story, began to hound the police, fueling public anxiety and speculation. Khan, feeling the weight of their expectations, redoubled his efforts, determined to bring the killer to justice.

He revisited the crime scene, examining every inch of the cell, searching for any overlooked clues. He noticed a small, almost imperceptible scratch on the wooden doorframe, a detail that had previously escaped his attention. Could it be a sign of forced entry? A desperate struggle? Or merely an insignificant mark?

Khan followed every lead, however faint, chasing shadows and pursuing dead ends. He interviewed every villager, from the elderly matriarch to the youngest child, searching for any inconsistencies, any hidden agendas. He meticulously analyzed every piece of evidence, searching for the elusive thread that would unravel the mystery.

But the killer remained elusive, a ghost in the shadows, leaving no trace, no footprints, no fingerprints. The village, once a vibrant community, was now paralyzed by fear, each resident a potential suspect, each shadow a potential threat. The idyllic Goan paradise had transformed into a nightmare, a chilling reminder of the darkness that lurked beneath the surface.

Inspector Khan, weary and disillusioned, found himself staring at the suicide note, the words "I take all the charge. XV." echoing in his mind. Was it truly a confession, or a desperate attempt to mislead the investigators?

He knew he had to find the truth, not just for the sake of justice, but also to bring peace back to the shattered community. The shadow of doubt hung heavy over the village, a constant reminder of the unanswered questions, the unresolved mystery. And as the days turned into weeks, Khan knew that the pressure to solve the case would only intensify, pushing him closer to the brink.

Inspector Khan, feeling the weight of their despair, knew he had to break the silence, to restore some semblance of normalcy to their lives. He organized community meetings, urging the villagers to share any information, however insignificant it might seem. He assured them that their safety was his priority, that he would do everything in his power to bring the killer to justice.

Slowly, tentatively, the villagers began to open. They shared their fears, their anxieties, their suspicions. A local fisherman claimed to have seen a strange boat lurking near the shore the night of the murder, a boat that had disappeared as quickly as it had appeared. A young girl reported hearing a muffled scream coming from the police station that night, but dismissed it as a nightmare.

Khan followed every lead, however tenuous, determined to sift through the rumors and uncover the truth. He interviewed the fisherman, who, despite his initial reluctance, provided a detailed description of the boat and its occupants. He questioned the young girl, trying to coax out more details about the scream, but she could only recall fragments of the terrifying sound.

The investigation led him to the neighboring village, the one with which Father Xavier had once been embroiled in a land dispute. Khan, frustrated by the lack of concrete evidence, decided to delve deeper into Father Xavier's personal life. He visited the church again, hoping to find any clues in the priest's belongings, any letters, any documents that might shed light on his past. He discovered a hidden compartment in Father Xavier's desk, containing a stack of old photographs and a single, cryptic letter.

The photographs depicted Father Xavier with a two young women, their faces etched with a tenderness that belied the priest's austere public persona. The letter, written in a foreign language, was addressed to

"my dearest Elena,"

Who was Elena? What was the nature of their relationship? And how did it connect to Father Xavier's murder? Khan, intrigued by the newfound information, embarked on a new line of inquiry, determined to unravel the mystery behind the enigmatic letter and the hidden photographs.

Khan was a bit eased having a name Elena but he was thinking who might be the second girl?

He sought the help of a local linguist to translate the letter. The translation revealed a poignant tale of love and loss, a forbidden romance that had been torn apart by societal pressures. Elena, it seemed, had been forced to marry another man, leaving Father Xavier heartbroken and disillusioned.

Could Elena, or someone connected to her, be involved in the murder? Was it a case of revenge, a long-buried grudge finally coming to fruition? Or was it a mere coincidence, a red herring leading him further astray?

Khan, his mind racing with possibilities, felt a surge of adrenaline. He knew he had to find Elena, to learn more about her life, her relationships, her past.

The search for Elena proved to be a daunting task. Years had passed since Father Xavier had written the letter, and there were no records of Elena in the village. Khan, however, refused to give up. He scoured old church records, interviewed elderly villagers, and followed every whisper, every rumor, hoping to find a trace of the woman who had once held such a significant place in Father Xavier's life.

The search for Elena led Khan to a remote village nestled in the foothills of the Western Ghats. There, he discovered that Elena, now an elderly woman, still resided in a small cottage, living a solitary life.

The meeting with Elena was both poignant and unsettling. The elderly woman, her eyes filled with a lifetime of sorrow, confirmed that she had indeed been deeply in love with Father Xavier. She spoke of a forbidden love, a love that had been cruelly snatched away from them, leaving an indelible mark on their lives.

However, Elena vehemently denied any involvement in Father Xavier's murder. She expressed her grief and shock at the news of his death, insisting that she had no enemies, no reason to harm him.

Khan, while acknowledging her sincerity, remained skeptical. He questioned her about her life after she had been forced to marry another man. He inquired about her family, her friends, her acquaintances, hoping to uncover any hidden connections, any potential motives.

Elena, despite her grief, was surprisingly forthcoming. She spoke of her unhappy marriage, her struggles to raise her children, her loneliness and despair. She revealed that she had kept in touch with Father Xavier over the years, exchanging letters and occasional visits.

Khan, intrigued by her revelations, delved deeper into her past, hoping to find any inconsistencies, any hidden agendas. He discovered that Elena had a son, a troubled young man Silas, who had been involved in a series of petty crimes. Could he be a potential suspect?

All of a sudden Khan remembered to ask about the other girl in the photograph too, he showed her the photograph. Elena broke up saying this was the last moment I captured with these TWINS. I don't know where she is now, she might be in London where she grew up. The only person loved by Xavier. No one noticed her as she was a weird looking girl. Her name is Julian….., but the official name is something Xavi used to tell me…in riddles.

''She is half of me

I am full of her

Together we share a name

Like…. A game''

This was the riddle khan and after this we clicked a picture. Oh! Those memories were awesome Khan, Thank you dear. May God bless you my child. May you find the killer of my Xavi.

Khan got a phone call from Rekha saying none of the bag fingerprint matches with Father Xavier. Khan was unhappy as he was thinking Father Xavier is the culprit but he got tangled again.

Suddenly another phone call from Rekha saying Sir, I have sent some images and this is more shocking, please check it out.

When Khan checked it was another bag named 'SANVI'.

Seeing the pictures, Khan left.

Chapter -11

FATHER XAVIER

The air in Seven Dials, London, hung thick with the cloying scent of coal smoke and damp cobblestones. It was a place where shadows danced in the labyrinthine alleyways, and whispers carried secrets as old as the city itself. Here, in a small, unassuming shop nestled amidst the clamor of street vendors and the rumble of horse-drawn carts, lived Xavier. Xavier was a man of small stature, his frame delicate, yet his presence commanded respect. His hands, though diminutive, were instruments of exquisite skill, capable of coaxing life back into broken clocks and transforming rough wood into intricate works of art. His face, etched with the lines of quiet contemplation, held a gentle intelligence. His eyes, a warm, deep brown, reflected the depth of his soul, holding stories untold. He possessed a quiet dignity, a strength born not of physical might, but of resilience and a profound understanding of the human heart.

His father, Mathew Xavier, was a stark contrast, a looming figure of power and fear. His broad shoulders and thick neck spoke of a life spent in the shadows, a life where violence was a language fluently spoken. His voice, a gravelly rumble, could silence a room, and his eyes, cold and calculating, held the weight of countless sins. He was a man of the underworld, a don whose influence stretched through the dark corners of London, a man who saw Xavier's gentleness as a weakness, a betrayal of the Xavier legacy.

Julian, Xavier's twin, was a mirror image of Mathew, a grotesque reflection of his father's brutality. Twins were short but not only shared the opposite character but also had opposite looks. They both shared a perfect bond. Julian always wanted to protect Xavi....but he was not interested in violence. Jerin Mathews, their elder brother who was killed by Mathew's enemies.

Their father always had a conversation with Jerin as he was framed exactly like him. Bad things follow us and take revenge in the most crucial times. Its burden is not taken by people who did crime but by their children....they bore the iniquity.

Then, Elena arrived, a breath of Andalusian sunshine in the perpetually grey London. She was a vision, her beauty a radiant beacon in the dimness of Seven Dials. Her skin, the color of warm honey, glowed with an inner light. Her hair, a cascade of raven silk, flowed down her back, framing a face of exquisite beauty. Her eyes, a vibrant emerald green, sparkled with intelligence and warmth, holding a depth of kindness that captivated all who met her. Elena worked as a seamstress in a nearby shop after college, her delicate fingers weaving magic with needle and thread.

Xavier, drawn to her like a moth to a flame, found himself captivated by her spirit. Their conversations, initially about the repair of the shop's clock, soon blossomed into deep discussions about art, literature, and the hidden beauty of the world. Elena saw beyond Xavier's physical appearance, recognizing the depth of his soul, the quiet strength that radiated from within. Their connection was a rare and precious thing, a bond forged in mutual respect and understanding.

However, Elena's family, steeped in tradition and fiercely protective of their daughter, saw Xavier's stature as an insurmountable barrier. Their disapproval was swift and harsh, their words laced with prejudice and a fear of societal judgment. "He is... incomplete," Elena's mother had hissed, her voice dripping with disdain. "He cannot provide for you, cannot give you the life you deserve." Her father, a stern man with eyes that held the weight of generations, echoed her sentiments. "He will bring shame upon our family, upon your name."

Elena, torn between her love for Xavier and her loyalty to her family, was caught in a cruel and impossible dilemma. Xavier, though heartbroken, understood their concerns. He knew that their love faced an uphill battle against the ingrained prejudices of their time. The rejection was a crushing blow, a stark reminder of the limitations society imposed upon him. It also made the hatred of his father grow stronger. Mathew blamed his son for the shame brought to the family, and Julian used the opportunity to further his own agenda, whispering poison into Mathew's ear.

The weight of his father's disdain, the venomous whispers of Julian, and the crushing pain of Elena's family's rejection made London a place of unbearable sorrow. Xavier felt the city closing in on him, its shadows mirroring the darkness that had settled in his heart.

Driven by a need for solace and a desperate yearning for a place where he could be accepted, Xavier left London. He chose Goa, a land of vibrant colors, fragrant spices, and a culture that seemed to embrace the beauty of diversity. The journey was long and arduous, a passage from the grey gloom of London to the sun-drenched shores of the Arabian Sea.

Goa welcomed him with open arms. The air, thick with the scent of jasmine and the salty tang of the sea, was a balm to his wounded soul. The vibrant colors of the markets, the rhythmic beat of the drums, and the gentle warmth of the Goan people were a stark contrast to the cold indifference of London.

He found a small, secluded cottage nestled amidst swaying palm trees, its walls painted in hues of ochre and saffron. He established a workshop, his skilled hands crafting intricate wooden carvings, drawing inspiration from the lush landscapes and the vibrant culture that surrounded him. He carved elephants with trunks raised in greeting, peacocks with feathers spread in dazzling display, and deities with serene expressions.

The Goan people, with their open hearts and accepting spirits, saw Xavier not as a man of small stature, but as a man of great skill and gentle wisdom. He became a respected member of the community, his carvings sought after for their beauty and craftsmanship. He found a sense of peace in the slower pace of life, the warmth of the sun, and the kindness of his new friends.

He never returned to London. The memories of Elena, the sting of rejection, and the coldness of his father and sister remained, but they faded with time, replaced by the gentle rhythm of his new life. He built a life of quiet contentment, surrounded by his art and the beauty of his adopted home. He never married, never had children, but he found a different kind of family in the people of Goa, a family that embraced him for who he was, a family that saw the beauty within.

The shadows of Seven Dials receded, replaced by the golden light of Goa. And in that golden light, Xavier found a measure of peace, a quiet acceptance that he had never found in the city of his birth.

Chapter 12

THE BEAR'S DEMISE

The humid air hung heavy in the late afternoon, thick with the scent of pine needles and damp earth. A small group of men, faces grim and determined, huddled around a weathered jeep, their eyes fixed on the dense wall of trees that marked the edge of the forbidden woods. Silas, his features etched with a lifetime of hardship, emerged from the vehicle, his movements fluid and practiced. Years spent hunting in these unforgiving wilds had honed his senses, making him as much a part of the forest as the creatures that dwelled within.

Silas, Elena's son, spent most of his time in Goa only, was a legend in these parts. Whispers of his exploits echoed through the local taverns – tales of a man who could track a deer through the deepest snow, who could outsmart the wariest of wolves, and who possessed an uncanny ability to anticipate the movements of his prey. Today, his prey was a different kind – a creature that had become a menace to the fragile peace of their small community.

Ash, a magnificent grizzly bear, had strayed far from its usual territory, drawn by the alluring scent of livestock and the promise of easy pickings. Its incursions had grown bolder, more frequent.

Fear had gripped the village, casting long shadows over their daily lives. Children were afraid to venture out alone, livestock were kept under constant guard, and the once-tranquil nights were now filled with the unsettling sounds of anxious whispers and the distant growl of the predator.

The news of the bear roaming and hunting hung in all media and a gripping fear hung in every area. Andrew asked Anthros after watching the news, are they talking about Ash, your pet. Anthros panicked. I can't lose him too. It's Silas, the hunter ... .call him.

Anthros ringed Silas but was unreachable.

He ran to the forest followed by Andrew.

The villagers, desperate for a solution, had turned to Silas. He was their last hope, their protector, the man who understood the ways of the wilderness better than anyone else. He had reluctantly agreed, the weight of responsibility heavy on his shoulders.

Silas, armed with a rifle passed down from his father, a weapon that had seen generations of hunters face down the wilderness, set off on his solitary quest. The forest, a labyrinth of interwoven branches and shadowed glades, swallowed him whole. He moved with the grace of a panther, his senses alert to every rustle of leaves, every snap of a twig. The air, heavy with the scent of pine needles, was now laced with the musky aroma of the bear, a potent blend of earth and animal.

He followed the trail, a grim testament to the bear's passage: trampled ferns, scattered patches of fur, and the unmistakable imprint of massive paws on the soft forest floor. The deeper he ventured, the more intense the bear's presence became. Silas felt a primal thrill course through him, a hunter's instinct awakening, a dance of predator and prey about to commence.

The sun, sinking below the horizon, cast long, eerie shadows that stretched and contorted, mimicking the hunter's own internal tension. The forest, once a vibrant tapestry of green, now seemed to hold its breath, anticipating the inevitable confrontation.

And then, he saw it.

The bear, a magnificent creature of raw power, emerged from a thicket of thorny bushes. Its fur, a patchwork of browns and grays, rippled with muscle as it moved, a testament to its immense strength. Its eyes, small and intelligent, surveyed the surroundings, assessing the threat. Silas, concealed behind a sturdy oak, held his breath, his heart pounding a frantic rhythm against his ribs.

The rifle, a familiar extension of his own arm, felt heavy in his hands. He aimed, his focus unwavering, his mind a blank canvas, devoid of all thoughts except the task at hand. The world seemed to shrink, the only reality was the sight through the scope, the bear, his target.

The shot echoed through the forest, a deafening explosion that shattered the tranquility. The bear, struck by the bullet, let out a roar that shook the very ground, a sound of pain and fury. It stumbled, its massive frame convulsing, then collapsed with a thunderous thud, its lifeblood staining the forest floor.

Silas, his hands trembling slightly, emerged from his hiding place. The air, thick with the acrid scent of gunpowder and the metallic tang of blood, hung heavy. A sense of satisfaction, primal and profound, washed over him. He had faced the danger, he had prevailed.

Yet, as he approached the fallen beast, a strange melancholy settled over him. The bear, despite its destructive tendencies, was a magnificent creature, a force of nature to be reckoned with. He felt a pang of respect for the raw power, the sheer will to survive that had driven this creature to the edge of human settlements.

The sound of voices broke through the silence. Inspector Abhishek, alerted by the gunshot, emerged from the surrounding thicket, their faces a mixture of relief and apprehension. They approached the fallen bear with a mixture of awe and trepidation, their eyes wide with the sheer scale of the creature.

As they drew closer, Inspector Abhishek noticed a small, metal tag dangling from the bear's ear. It read, "ASH." A wave of realization washed over him. This was not just a rogue bear; this was Anthros's pet.

Anthros cried loudly and hugged him tightly. Anthros screamed Hospital....... He is still breathing. Andrew, seeing his brother crying, hugged Anthros. Two of the cubs came behind the bush, Ash was protecting its children. Ash plucked out the tag and gave it to Anthros before its final gasping. Andrew picked one of the cubs and named one ASH, witnessed by Ash. He asked forgiveness of his deed.

Abhishek arranged for an ambulance and took Ash.

It is humans who can't forgive each other but animals are not like that, if we love them they will love till their last breath.

Anthros, a renowned wildlife conservationist, had rescued this bear cub years ago, nurturing it back to health and releasing it back into the wild. The bear, imprinted on Anthros, had always returned to his care, a testament to the deep bond they shared.

Anthros, inconsolable, demanded to know who was responsible. Whispers and accusations flew, but Silas remained silent. The weight of his actions, the realization that he had not just killed a dangerous animal but a beloved companion, weighed heavily on his conscience.

Ash breathed his last in the hospital. Anthros and Andrew gave Ash a beautiful burial, and now Ash has given them two souls to love and cherish. Anthros was happy to see Andrews change but was a bit scared of his hidden nature.

The truth of bear's killer was out, it was none other than his best friend Silas and his gang, however, it was far more complex than a simple man-versus-beast conflict. Silas and Anthros, once inseparable friends, had fallen out bitterly. A college prank, a morphed photograph, a cruel joke taken too far – the incident had festered, turning friendship into enmity. The anger, bottled up for years, had found an unexpected outlet in the hunt.

Silas, haunted by the memory of his friendship with Anthros, the guilt gnawing at his conscience, remained silent, his secret buried deep within his heart. The forest, once a source of solace, now held a bitter echo of his past, a constant reminder of the consequences of his actions.

Anthros didn't say a word and said let all the killings be finished with me itself. It is difficult to break a tradition. One has to stand firm and say NO, though NO is a powerful word but it carries a series of consequences.

Chapter 13

DIGGING THE TRUTH

Inspector Khan, weary-eyed and burdened by the weight of the recent bear death case, hands over the investigation to his capable subordinate, Inspector Abhishek. Khan, though relieved to be off the gruesome case, still carries the lingering unease of the unsolved mystery.

Khan's attention now turns to a different, yet equally disturbing, series of events: the disappearance of several female students from the prestigious St. Xavier's College. The common thread in these cases is the discovery of one pristine white pillows, each bearing an unsettlingly perfect imprint of a human face, devoid of any discernible features.

Khan's doubt leads him to Professor Mishael Mathew, an enigmatic figure shrouded in an aura of both fascination and fear. She is a dwarf, her stature dwarfed by the towering buildings of the campus, yet her presence commands attention. Her eyes, a startling shade of emerald green, hold a depth of emotion that belies her diminutive frame.

Mishael Mathew is a beloved figure among the students, known for her quirky humor, unconventional teaching methods, and unwavering support. However, beneath the jovial exterior lies a deep-seated melancholy, a shadow cast by a lifelong struggle with mood disorders.

Whispers begin to circulate among the faculty and students, fueled by fear and fueled by the chilling discovery of the blood stains in the basement. Khan, a seasoned investigator, approaches Mishael Mathew with caution. He observes her closely, noting her every reaction, every subtle shift in her demeanor. He delves into her past, interviewing former colleagues, students, and even her estranged family members, seeking any clues that might link her to the disappearances.

As the investigation progresses, a chilling pattern emerges. Several witnesses report sightings of a shadowy figure lurking around the campus at night, a figure that seems to vanish into thin air. The students whisper of a "Nighttime Prowler," a tall man, a malevolent entity that preys upon the unsuspecting.

The discovery of the latest victim, a young woman named Sanvi found brutally murdered in her dorm room, sends shockwaves through the campus. The scene of the crime is eerily reminiscent of the pillow imprints, a chilling tableau of violence and despair.

Khan's investigation takes a surprising turn. He remembers this is the same Sanvi whose bag has been opened by Rekha, he rushed towards Rekha for the truth but she left for a vacation.

He discovers a series of disturbing diary entries penned by Xavier's, the same handwriting, filled with dark fantasies, violent imagery, and a disturbing obsession with the students. The entries reveal a hidden side consumed by a deep-seated rage and a twisted desire for control.

He continuously contacted Rekha but of no use, suddenly the picture which he found in Father's room fell down from his diary. He sends Abhishek to photoshop the picture and make it around 50 -60 years.

He calls the cyber cell and hand-over them the Professor's number to track down the details of her movement. The whole night he was thinking of Xavier and Julian…and in the dusk he got a phone call from Elena

Hello!

Is it Khan? I am Elena. Remember you met me. Yes tell me Mrs Elena…

Khan, I solved the riddle.

It's 'Reivax'.

"She is half of me

I am full of her

Together we share a name

Like…. A game"

Just Like game…..

Check your phone I have messaged you the spelling, If you find her tell her I still remember her.

She cuts the call.

Khan checks the message…

"XAVIER = REIVAX"

Khan thought what is the point, Jesus?! Abhishek brings the photograph and as Khan checks it….

Khan gets thrilled seeing this…..and as he understood it was Mishael Mathew. Uff Julian… The REIVAX.

He said Thank You Jesus now everything has a point.

God's direction is perfect, we just need to follow it.

Khan rushed towards the college. He checks the register, handwriting it was all the same... .Twin has taken advantage.

Khan begins to watch Reivax, driven by a combination of her mental illness, a deep-seated resentment towards the students, and a twisted desire to know, the "Nighttime Prowler." He believes she preys upon the students at night, driven by a dark compulsion to exert control over their lives.

Khan uncovers the chilling details of Reivax's modus operandi, by continuously following her. He discovers that she targets her victims, primarily young women, while they sleep. She then proceeds to torture them, inflicting unimaginable pain, before ultimately taking their lives. The act of peeling off their nails, a gruesome detail that emerges from the investigation, becomes a chilling signature of her crimes. There is a tall person who helps her. The person in the shadow.

Khan, driven by a sense of urgency and fueled by a growing sense of dread, launches a manhunt for Reivax. He mobilizes his team, scouring the campus and surrounding areas, searching for any trace of the elusive professor.

The chase leads them through a labyrinth of hidden tunnels beneath the campus, a network of forgotten passages that Reivax has used to conceal her victims. The atmosphere is thick with tension, the silence broken only by the pounding of their hearts and the echoing footsteps of the pursuers.

The humid air hung thick and heavy, a suffocating blanket mirroring the tension in Inspector Khan's gut. He'd been trailing "Julian" for days, a phantom figure leaving a trail of cryptic clues and unsettling disappearances. From his vantage point, a dilapidated warehouse across the docks, Khan observed the figure moving with a predator's grace, a silhouette against the flickering neon signs reflecting off the murky water. He raised his binoculars, focusing on the figure's movements, the subtle shifts in posture, the almost imperceptible tension in the shoulders. Something was off. This wasn't the calculated precision he'd associated with her. There was a raw, almost feral energy radiating from the figure.

Suddenly, a cold dread washed over Khan. He felt a prickling sensation on the back of his neck, a sense of being watched. He turned, but it was too late. A figure, swift and silent as a viper, emerged from the shadows, a cloth clamped over his mouth,injected sedative in his neck. The world spun, the dock lights blurring into a dizzying kaleidoscope, and then, nothing.

Khan awoke to the sting of salt and the metallic tang of blood. He was bound, his wrists and ankles secured with rough rope, the coarse fibers digging into his skin. The dim light of a single bare bulb revealed the interior of a shipping container, a cold, metallic tomb. His head throbbed, and his vision swam, but the figure standing before him was chillingly clear.

"Welcome, Inspector Khan," a voice, smooth and laced with a chilling amusement, echoed in the confined space. The figure stepped into the light, and Khan's breath hitched. It was a woman, the Professor standing on a stilt, her features sharp and predatory, her eyes gleaming with a cruel intelligence. "I believe you were expecting someone else?"

"Reivax," Khan rasped, the name a bitter taste on his tongue. He'd heard whispers of her, a tall man, shadowy figure operating in the underbelly of the city, a master manipulator, a ghost. He'd dismissed the rumors as exaggerated tales, but now, facing her, he knew the truth.

"Clever boy," Reivax purred, a predatory smile stretching across her lips. "Yes, I am Reivax. And you, Inspector, have been a persistent little fly. I decided it was time to swat you."

The beating that followed was brutal, a calculated assault designed to break not just his body, but his spirit. Reivax moved with a terrifying efficiency, each blow precise, each strike aimed to inflict maximum pain. Khan gritted his teeth, refusing to give her the satisfaction of a scream. He knew he was close to the edge, his vision blurring, his body screaming in protest. He challenged her to untie her ropes but as she was above to hit him last...

Just as darkness threatened to consume him, a sudden commotion erupted outside the container. The sound of shouting, the thud of heavy footsteps, and the sharp crack of gunfire pierced the air. The container door burst open, revealing the silhouette of a figure, gun drawn.

"Khan!" Abhishek's voice, strained but determined, cut through the chaos. He'd been tracking Khan's movements, a digital trail leading him to the docks. He'd sensed something was wrong, a sudden disruption in Khan's signal, and had followed his instincts.

The ensuing firefight was a blur of motion and sound. Abhishek, a seasoned officer, moved with a practiced precision, his shots finding their mark. Reivax, caught off guard, retreated into the shadows, disappearing as quickly as she had appeared.

Abhishek rushed to Khan's side, quickly cutting through the ropes binding him. Khan, battered and bruised, leaned against Abhishek, his breath ragged. "Reivax," he gasped, "not Mishael Mathew. It was Reivax."

Finally, Khan and his team corner Reivax in a hidden chamber deep within the tunnels. The confrontation is intense, a battle of wills between the seasoned investigator and the deranged professor. Reivax, cornered and desperate, unleashes a torrent of rage, a final, desperate act of defiance. Khan again got a blow on his head making him unconscious and as she was about to kill Abhishek shot from behind, gaining the consciousness of Khan. They together caught hold of her and arrested her.

This culminates in a dramatic showdown, a final confrontation that leaves both Khan and Reivax scarred. The truth is finally revealed, the darkness that had lurked beneath the surface of the seemingly idyllic campus brought to light. Reivax ends with a sense of lingering unease, the echoes of the tragedy resonating long after the dust has settled.

She is taken into custody for further interrogation and investigation.

Chapter 14

"TRUTH FROM THE LIPS OF THE HUNTER."

The flickering torchlight cast long, dancing shadows across the damp stone walls of the dungeon. Rain lashed against the barred window, mirroring the storm raging within me. Years of secrets, of guilt, of living a lie, were finally tumbling out, confessions wrung from the depths of my soul.

The confessions started in hours and ended in days. Inspector Khan who had bandage every wound and Abhishek was already shocked hearing her brutality, confessing like a leaf fallen from the tree. No pain and no flickering of eyes.

Reivax, the name still tasted like ash on my tongue. It was a name I had buried deep, a persona I had carefully constructed to shield myself from the truth. But the truth, like a venomous snake, had finally coiled around me, its fangs poised to strike.

Jealousy, that insidious green-eyed monster, had been the genesis of my descent. Mary, with her radiant smile and effortless grace, had always been a thorn in my side. Her presence, a constant reminder of the beauty I lacked, the love I craved. And so, I had taken her from him, from Xavi, extinguishing her light, leaving him shrouded in an eternal darkness and making him realize that I am beautiful too. I always wanted to marry Xavi, I know it's wrong…it's wrong… don't stare at me like that. I am not beautiful but I want to marry..no one will marry me..she started sobbing… as time passed by I started falling for Xavi…he was always there for me but before I could say a word, Xavi was found with Elena. I only showed my father you know…rest you found out Khan.

Khan realizing the brutality, he showed the list of girls missing typed on a paper. These names I found written on 'THE PILLOWS'

Do you know these girls? Khan started reading loudly

1. Swizel Sebastein
2. Sandra Varghese
3. Mary Alphonzo
4. Grace Rozario
5. Amelia Varghese
6. Diana Joseph
7. Anna Jacob
8. Victoria
9. Anna Jose
10. Shelial Fernandez

I know all of them….some of the names I forgot…

You didn't get any boys… Oh! Khan there are more pillows.

I killed my father first as I told him about my love towards Xavi, he started moral lectures, the whole life he was the blood shedder and suddenly giving moral lectures wasn't acceptable.

Khan I took hold of him from behind and strangled him to death…… I made his bone pebbles and crushed them in the grinder and smoothened them and instead of feathers, I stuffed pebbles. Everyday night, I talk to him just like he talk to my older brother Jerin.

Look he is there standing and listening...

Abhishek got scared.

Then comes Swizel, the arrogant noblewoman, who had paid the ultimate price for her cruelty, for her disdain. My hatred for her, fueled by years of simmering resentment, had consumed me. I had become a monster, my hands stained with the blood of the innocent. She was close with Xavi, I observed her from far. She was in love with Xavier. A nine year old falling in love with a teacher.

Angel, her sister, the only survivor, a constant, haunting reminder of my crimes. I had spared her life, a twisted act of mercy, a desperate attempt to cling to the last vestiges of my humanity. But more than that, I had kept her alive to protect the secret I had sworn to uphold. Angel knew my secret as she had seen me in the darkest of the night. The students who come for Sunday school and guitar lessons I used to trick them and make them vanish. She saw me taking away Mary. She followed me everywhere. I never hunted her as I know she will not reveal it to anyone. No one will trust her. I always knew that kidnapping the little girls is easy but as Xavier is gone, who provided me with a motive to hunt, so I shifted my hunt to college because I can't control my hunting. This brings me passion to the dark world. Abhishek raised his hand but stopped by Khan.

Reivax said, my face ... .don't you dare.

My brother, my love Xavi, Father Xavier, the only confidante I had ever known. He, with his gentle eyes and unwavering faith, had been the anchor in the tempest of my soul. He had always seen the darkness within me, the monster lurking beneath the surface. Yet, he had never condemned me, never turned away.

"You carry the character of our father, Michael Xavier," his words echoed in the chilling silence of the dungeon. "He was a cunning fellow, a master manipulator." My father, a specter haunting the corridors of my memory. A man of shadows, a master of deceit. He had rejected me well, the art of manipulation, the thrill of the hunt, as if he agreed that I am the monster and man-eater of this house. But his rejections had come at a terrible cost. I never knew my mother.

Every sin, every act of violence, had been a confession whispered in the darkness. I would seek out my brother, hand him a pillow, and pour out my soul, the weight of my guilt momentarily lifted by his silent understanding. He would listen, without judgment, his eyes filled with a profound sorrow. He never checked those Pillows because all carried the smell of lavender flowers.

But that night, the night of reckoning, had shattered the fragile peace we had forged. I had visited him in the cell, desperate, seeking absolution. I had begged him to take the burden upon himself, to shield me from the consequences of my actions. But he had refused.

"I will tell the truth," he hissed, his voice a venomous serpent. "I will expose you for the monster you truly are."

I repeatedly said that I am in love with you, I will bring you out of this. But he disagreed.

And so, I had made my choice. I had silenced him, forever, hanging him from the very rafters of the cell. The weight of his betrayal, the betrayal of the only man who had ever truly known me, had crushed me.

Now, months later, the truth was finally spilling out, a torrent of guilt and remorse washing over me. The hunter had become the hunted, the predator now caged, his prey the merciless justice that awaited him.

Inspector Khan asked what you did with those bodies. She said she crushed it in the crusher and those pebbles are not pebbles, they are bones. CARVED AND PAINTED. Oh! How will you know? I told Rekha not to reveal that part. She will reach today from her vacation. Khan got fueled in anger and gave a tight slap under her cheeks saying. This slap is from Father Xavier.

Reivax fell down and started crying like a child.

Abhishek continued "Who was the helper for all this as I know, this is impossible for you to do alone! exclaimed Abhishek. Reivax smirked and said it was Raghothri who helped all this but I haven't been able to see him for the past few days.

Khan said…oh…nice I killed him. He murmured.

Who was the other person? Khan asked vaguely. A quick answer from her, find it Khan you are a smart fellow. It is one among you. He is more psychic than me, people think that all those who kill are psychic, I was not like that I can be normal and psychic at the same time. But he is a common man but actually a psychic.

Fear gripped in Khan and in control he asked the next question.

All these girls used to giggle with Xavi, as I used to watch from far. I used to get angry.

Khan, Jesus was the most innocent God on the earth yet he was crucified, you know why? He was betrayed by his Judas. Thank God Jesus rose again to prove everything wrong. He still loved all.

My family, my father the great Don clearly showed the path of betrayal even though I was born ugly Khan they could have loved me, I wouldn't be the bad person. See Xavi he turned to God because my father had no compassion for him. I turned to the way of Cain, you know Cain right the first murderer in the Bible.

I was the blank slate for my father he could have filled with flowers but he chose harsh words.

Khan had no words at first but he said one thing, I am a Muslim and a Christian, I know not much about Jesus Christ but I know one thing as you said Reivax, word has the power to change everything and you are the one who, to prove yourself.

DON'T CHANGE THE WORDS OF THE BIBLE TO PROVE YOURSELF RIGHT.

Killing and abusing anyone is not a solution or revenge to what your Father did to you.

Reivax slammed for a while and said Mary who giggled with Xavi, was it right?

But Killing was not the answer, shouted Khan…..

Jesus is not a soap that you can do anything and rely on for cleanliness. He shed HIS precious blood for us so that we don't shed the blood of anyone anymore. HE TAUGHT US

FORGIVENESS, But humans are full of vengeance, what they don't like they get rid off.

Khan was about to hit her again, but was interrupted by higher officials.

Reivax replied my brother told me once about you, you who carry both cultures in your veins didn't let that hit your brain. Your father taught you well and that brings a fine personality in you, whatever our ancestors do the generations suffer ... What are you expecting from me and from my family? Don't you think Xavi didn't get angry, he hid everything but his love was taken away from him. She was pulled behind.....but Khan left the place.

The flickering torchlight cast long, dancing shadows across the damp stone walls of the dungeon. Rain lashed against the barred window, mirroring the storm raging within me. The end was near, I knew it. But as I awaited my fate, a chilling realization dawned upon me: true justice, I had discovered, was far more terrifying than any punishment I could have imagined..

Inspector Abhishek handed him his phone showing him the picture of Father Xavier suicidal note letter named RV. It was written by her. The cunning girl, mastermind of all this.

Chapter 15

THE CASE IS CLOSED

The culmination of weeks of relentless investigation finally arrived. Inspector Khan, his face etched with a mixture of relief and exhaustion, stood in the courtroom, the weight of his sister's tragic demise finally lifted, albeit partially. The courtroom, a somber tableau of justice, held the accused: Anthony, his face pale and drawn, and Professor Reivax, his demeanor a chilling mix of defiance and despair.

The judge, his voice firm and measured, pronounced the verdict. Anthony, found guilty of conspiracy and aiding in the murder of his wife, was sentenced to ten years of rigorous imprisonment. A collective gasp rippled through the courtroom as the judge turned to Professor Reivax. His voice resonated with gravity as he declared the sentence: death by hanging. The courtroom fell silent, the weight of the verdict hanging heavy in the air. Professor Reivax, his face contorted in a grotesque mask of disbelief and rage, uttered a string of incoherent curses before being led away by the guards.

A wave of relief washed over Inspector Khan, a fragile sense of closure finally settling over him. He glanced towards his partner,

Inspector Abhishek, their eyes meeting in a silent exchange of understanding and shared triumph. The courtroom, previously tense and charged with anticipation, erupted in a spontaneous round of applause. The public, who had followed the case with rapt attention, acknowledged the dedication and perseverance of the investigating officers.

Silas, the game hunter, was not spared the consequences of his actions. Found guilty of aiding and abetting the murder, he was sentenced to two years of imprisonment and a hefty fine of Rs1,50,000/-. The courtroom buzzed with murmurs of satisfaction as the judge delivered the verdict. Justice, however belated, had been served.

Judge requested the forensic team to handover all those pillows which had been ruled out, to their parents, as their souls were crushed. Let them bury and pray for those lost souls.

The spotlight then shifted to Andrew and Anthros. Their names, once synonymous with suspicion and fear, were now cleared. The accusations against them, born from a web of deceit and manipulation, had crumbled under the weight of evidence. As the judge declared them innocent, a palpable sense of joy filled the courtroom. Andrew and Anthros, their faces etched with relief and disbelief, embraced each other, tears streaming down their faces. The years of living under the shadow of suspicion, the constant fear of imprisonment, had finally dissipated. They were free.

The courtroom, a microcosm of the human experience, had witnessed the triumph of justice, the fragility of human life, and the enduring power of truth. As the final verdict was delivered, the courtroom slowly emptied, each individual carrying with them the echoes of the trial, the weight of the verdict, and the bittersweet taste of closure.

Inspector Khan, his mind still reeling from the events of the day, stepped out of the courtroom into the crisp evening air. The weight of the investigation, the relentless pursuit of the truth, had taken its toll. He felt a profound sense of emptiness, a void left by the loss of his sister. The conviction of the perpetrators, while a necessary step towards justice, couldn't erase the pain of her absence.

He called his father in a church to tell the truth about his sister. He asked Abhiskek to contact all the parents who have lost their children and handover those pillows. Abhishek did so.

He met with Abhishek outside the courthouse. "It's over, Abhishek," Khan said, his voice hoarse with emotion.

"Yes, sir, but still the helper." Abhishek replied, his eyes reflecting a similar weariness. "We brought them to partial justice."

Abhishek, understanding the depth of his partner's grief, placed a hand on his shoulder. "We did everything we could, sir. We found the half truth."

Khan nodded, his gaze softening. "You were instrumental, Abhishek. Your dedication, your sharp mind... they were invaluable. Thank you for saving me."

"Thank you, sir," Abhishek replied, a genuine smile gracing his lips. "It was a team effort."

They stood in silence for a moment, the weight of the day settling over them. Then, Khan turned to him. "Go home, Abhishek. You deserve some rest."

"You too, sir," Abhishek replied, before turning to leave.

Khan watched him go, a wave of exhaustion washing over him. He needed his family to find solace in their company. But as he walked away from the courthouse, he couldn't shake off the feeling that the shadow of his sister's death would forever linger, a constant reminder of the fragility of life and the enduring power of evil. It was her half-pillow that brought the truth so far. She was watching me all the time, I hoped I would have been there when she vanished. Khan sobbed under the tree.

Meanwhile, Andrew and Anthros, their freedom finally secured, were overwhelmed with emotion. They had spent years living under the constant threat of imprisonment, their lives consumed by fear and suspicion. The accusations, born from a web of lies and deceit, had shattered their lives, tearing them apart from their families and friends.

Now, as they walked out of the courthouse, the world felt different. The air seemed fresher, the sunlight brighter. They embraced, tears of joy streaming down their faces.

"We're free," Andrew whispered, his voice trembling with emotion. "We're finally free."

"Yes," Anthros replied, his voice thick with emotion. "We'll rebuild our lives, Andrew. We'll find happiness again."

They spent the next few hours simply enjoying their freedom, walking through the park, savoring the taste of freedom, the feeling of the sun on their faces. They knew the road to recovery would be long and arduous, but they were determined to rebuild their lives, to find joy and happiness once again.

The case of the murdered heiress had finally come to an end. Justice, however imperfect, had been served. But the scars of the tragedy, the pain and suffering it had inflicted, would linger long after the courtroom doors had closed.

Anthros met Khan and they hugged each other. Anthros asked him about Rekha. He said I found her. She is ok but her mother is on a ventilator. The brutality was taken upon the mother, she escaped.

You enjoy Anthros dear, May your bond increase. Take care of your brother.

Chapter 16

KNOWING ABOUT JESUS CHRIST

The clang of the cell door echoed through the stale air of the prison, a jarring sound that punctuated the monotony of Reivax's confinement. Days blurred into weeks, each one a grim reminder of her descent into a life of crime. Loneliness gnawed at her, a constant, gnawing companion in the stifling confines of her cell.

One afternoon, a tall, imposing figure materialized in the doorway. Pastor William Samuel, a man whose presence exuded an aura of quiet strength, had come to visit the inmates. He moved through the rows of cells, his gaze steady and compassionate as he offered words of comfort and hope.

As he approached Reivax's cell, she noticed the lines etched on his face, a testament to years spent ministering to the lost and forgotten. He spoke of Jesus Christ, his voice resonating with a profound conviction that captivated Reivax's attention.

"Jesus," Pastor William explained, "is the way, the truth, and the life. He offers forgiveness and redemption to all who believe in him."

Reivax listened intently, a flicker of curiosity igniting within her. She had heard of Jesus before, fleeting mentions in hushed conversations and distant prayers. But this was different. Pastor William spoke with such sincerity, such unwavering faith, that his words began to seep into the hardened corners of her heart.

She was thinking of Khan's words, Jesus is not a soap that you can do anything and rely on for cleanliness. He shed HIS precious blood for us so that we don't shed the blood of anyone anymore. But humans are full of vengeance, what they don't like they get rid off. HE TAUGHT US FORGIVENESS.

Yet, a nagging doubt lingered. "Why didn't Jesus stop me from sinning?" she asked, her voice trembling slightly. "Why didn't he change my mind when I was committing those crimes?"

Pastor William paused, his gaze softening. ''Dear," he said gently, "Jesus offers us freedom, but he never forces it upon us. We are free to choose our own paths, to embrace or reject his love. If you truly enjoy sin, if you find pleasure in the darkness, you will be trapped. You will crave more, always wanting more."

His words struck a chord deep within her. Reivax had always felt a strange emptiness, a void that she tried to fill with illicit gains and fleeting pleasures. But those pleasures had only brought her to this desolate place, a prisoner of her own desires.

Pastor William continued, "Jesus gives us warnings. He sends people into our lives, people who witness our sins and try to guide us back to the light. But often, we choose to ignore them, to bury our heads in the sand and pretend that everything is fine."

He recounted stories of individuals who had been confronted with their wrongdoing, yet stubbornly clung to their sinful ways, blinded by their own pride and self-deception. Reivax listened, her heart heavy with the weight of her own transgressions.

For the first time, a genuine sense of guilt washed over her. The facade of bravado she had built around herself began to crumble, revealing the vulnerable, broken woman beneath. Tears welled up in her eyes, tears of remorse, of regret, of a newfound awareness of her own sinfulness.

"Help me," she whispered, her voice choking with emotion. "Help me find my way back."

Pastor William's face lit up with a radiant smile. "Dear," he said, his voice filled with hope, "it's never too late. Jesus' arms are always open. All you need to do is turn to him, confess your sins, and ask for his forgiveness. He will welcome you back with open arms, embrace you with his love, and set you free."

Reivax, bathed in the soft glow of the flickering lamplight, felt a glimmer of hope, a fragile seed of faith taking root in the barren soil of her despair.

The encounter with Pastor William left an indelible mark on Reivax. His words echoed in her mind, haunting her with their truth and challenging her deeply ingrained beliefs. She began to reflect on her life, on the choices she had made, and the consequences that followed.

She remembered a time, long ago, when she was a young girl, filled with dreams and aspirations. She had envisioned a life of purpose, of making a positive impact on the world. But somewhere along the way, she had strayed from that path, lured by the allure of easy killings and the thrill of the forbidden.

She thought about the people she had hurt, the lives she had disrupted, the pain she had inflicted on others. Guilt gnawed at her, a constant, unrelenting companion. The joy and excitement she had once experienced in her criminal activities had long since faded, replaced by a deep sense of emptiness and despair.

Reivax began to see the truth in Pastor William's words. She had indeed been warned, countless times. Her Xavi had pleaded with her to change her ways, to abandon her life of crime.

Now, the memory of that terrified child haunted her. She realized that her actions had not only impacted her own life but had also caused immense suffering to others. The weight of her sins felt unbearable, crushing her spirit and leaving her feeling utterly lost and alone.

Days turned into weeks, and weeks into months. Reivax spent her days in quiet contemplation, wrestling with her past and grappling with the possibility of redemption. She read the Bible, which Pastor William had kindly provided, and found solace in its words of comfort and hope.

She began to see the world through a different lens. The petty grievances, the anger, the resentment that had fueled her actions began to fade, replaced by a growing sense of compassion and understanding. She started to see the interconnectedness of all beings, the impact of her actions on the lives of others.

One day, as she was reading the Bible, a verse struck her with profound force:

"Blessed is the one who does not walk in the path of the wicked." She repented in the cell crying out loud, remembering killing her own twin. The love of her life.

Reivax decided to take the first step towards redemption. She began to reach out to the victims of her crimes, seeking forgiveness for the pain she had caused. It was a humbling experience, filled with fear and trepidation. She wrote letters addressing Khan and decided to give it when the last day comes.

Reivax began to attend church services regularly inside the cell, finding solace and strength in the community of believers. She participated in Bible studies, shared her testimony with others, but all giggled and made fun of her. But she didn't say a word.

She also volunteered at a local soup kitchen, serving meals to the homeless and needy. The act of helping others brought her a sense of purpose and fulfillment that she had never experienced before.

As time passed, Reivax began to feel a profound transformation within herself. The anger, the bitterness, the resentment that had consumed her for so long began to dissipate, replaced by a newfound sense of peace and tranquility.

She felt a deep connection to something greater than herself, a sense of belonging to a larger purpose. She had found a new life, a life filled with meaning and purpose, a life dedicated to making amends and spreading love and compassion.

Reivax's transformation was remarkable. She became a beacon of hope for other inmates, sharing her testimony and offering guidance and support. She helped organize Bible studies within the prison, offering a lifeline of hope to those struggling with despair and hopelessness, a new journey with the Saviour.

She also became an advocate for prison reform, working tirelessly to improve conditions for inmates and to provide them with opportunities for rehabilitation and reintegration into society, but many mocked seeing a tiny creature telling about redemption of sins.

Reivax's journey was not without its challenges. There were times when doubt crept in, when the weight of her past threatened to overwhelm her. But she clung to her faith, drawing strength from the words of Pastor William and the support of her newfound community.

She learned that forgiveness was not just about seeking absolution from others but also about forgiving herself. She learned to embrace her past, not as a source of shame and regret, but as a catalyst for growth and transformation.

Reivax's life became a living testament to the power of redemption. She had been a prisoner of her own desires, bound by the chains of sin. But through faith, forgiveness, and a commitment to personal growth, she had broken free from those chains, emerging as a transformed individual. The. Day arrived.

Chapter 17

THE FINAL

The deathroom was heavy with the weight of the ending. Reivax, her face pale and drawn, sat rigidly in the death chair. The judge's voice, though firm, death by hanging was echoing in the ears.

A wave of emotions, a chaotic symphony of despair and disbelief, washed over Reivax. Her mind raced, a whirlwind of thoughts and regrets. The crimes she had committed, the lives she had irrevocably altered – the weight of it all pressed down on her. Yet, amidst the turmoil, a flicker of peace emerged. She had found solace in Jesus Christ, a beacon of light in the encroaching darkness.

I was the terror outside but after coming here, I understood all are terror in their own life only they are masking it. I have evidenced it in nights, everynight these ugly women tear me apart. They were like hunted hyenas lurking for blood. I remembered how I used to enjoy the screams of innocent and see Xavi ... .look ,Xavi, they enjoy mine. Reivax said, looking at the picture of Xavi. But see Xavi, I found peace in the Bible.

The revelation had come unexpectedly, a profound shift in her perspective. The world, once a canvas of chaos and self-gratification, now appeared in a new light. She saw the interconnectedness of all beings, the sanctity of life. This newfound understanding brought a measure of tranquility, a sense of purpose even in the face of impending doom.

However, the tranquility was fleeting. The stark reality of her sentence – the finality of death – began to sink in. A desperate yearning for life, a primal instinct for survival, surged within her. She yearned to experience the world anew, to witness the beauty of a sunrise, to feel the warmth of the sun on her skin, to taste the sweetness of a ripe fruit.

The weight of her crimes, however, cast a long shadow. The atrocities she had committed – the manipulation, the deceit, the calculated acts of violence – were a heavy burden to bear. Guilt gnawed at her, a constant, unrelenting companion. Could she ever truly atone for the pain she had inflicted? Could she find forgiveness, not just from others, but from herself? No one can save me now, Ah! How they will I killed my own blood and rest who pleaded for life were killed forever.

The afternoon of her execution arrived, the sun casting long shadows across the prison grounds. Reivax, clad in a simple white gown, was led to the gallows, her steps heavy with resignation. As the noose tightened around her neck, a single tear escaped her eye. It was a tear of sorrow, of regret, how he killed Xavi, her own brother.

In that final moment, her thoughts turned to the teachings of Christ – love, forgiveness, and redemption. She closed her eyes, seeking solace in the divine, her spirit transcending the confines of her earthly existence.

Before she could step, Khan came in and asked, I wanted to know why you left Mary's half body in Anthony's house. She opened her eyes and said I wanted to kill her and grind her but it was witnessed by Angel. Nice you came, I Knew you will, please under my Bible are the letters for the families, please give them Khan. I will never forget you.

She closed her eyes, her face was covered.

The executioner pulled the lever. The trapdoor swung open. Reivax's life, a tumultuous journey marked by darkness and fleeting moments of light, came to an abrupt end.

The dwarf tales, the chronicle of her life, both tragic and triumphant, were now closed. Reivax, the enigmatic figure who had captivated and terrified, was no more. Whereas Xavi who continuously wanted her sister to pull out of hell, was killed by his own blood.

People kill their own blood to find freedom but in reality these deeds are bringing curse to the coming generations.

Yet, her story, a cautionary tale of ambition and its consequences, lingered, a stark reminder of the fragility of life and the importance of choosing compassion over cruelty.

Khan who was thunderstruck by the revelation of Angel, knowing everything and being quiet led him to an amazement.

Chapter -18

ECHOES OF MARY, SHADOWS OF THE HELPER

The sterile scent of antiseptic and lemon polish did little to soothe the turmoil within Khan. Reivax's revelations, a relentless torrent of truths she couldn't fully decipher, had left him shattered. Mary… buried, but still haunted. The phrase echoed in Khan's mind, a chilling whisper that refused to be silenced.

He took all the letters from the cell and reading them one by one made him panic.

Dr. Anya Sharma, his counselor, adjusted her spectacles, her gaze gentle yet probing. "Khan, you're fixating on this phrase. 'Buried, but still haunted.' What does it mean to you?"

Khan clenched her hands, the smooth leather of the chair digging into her palms. "It… it's like a ghost. Mary… she was a part of me, a part of everything. Reivax said… things those letters. Terrible things. And now, even though… Even though she's gone, it feels like she's still here. Like her influence, her... her presence is still poisoning everything."

"Poisoning?" Dr. Sharma's voice was soft, encouraging.

"Yes! The secrets, the lies... they're like a rot spreading through my life." Khan's voice rose, a tremor of fear lacing his words. "And the helper... that constant, lurking presence. I can feel him, even now. Watching. Waiting. He's like a shadow, always just at the edge of my vision."

The "helper," a figure Reivax had alluded to, was a constant source of dread. He was a puppeteer, pulling strings Khan couldn't see, manipulating events from the shadows. His "luring around" was no mere coincidence; it was a calculated dance, a predator circling its prey.

The counselling sessions were a fragile lifeline, a brief respite from the suffocating weight of his reality. Dr. Sharma helped him to unpack the tangled threads of his past, the fragmented memories that surfaced like shards of broken glass. But even in the sanctuary of the office, Khan felt the helper's gaze, a cold, unseen presence that made his skin crawl.

One evening, after a particularly draining session, Khan decided to confront his fear. He knew he couldn't run forever. He walked the familiar path home, but this time, he was acutely aware of every shadow, every rustle of leaves. He stopped at the edge of the park, the place where he'd first felt the helper's presence, and turned, his voice a defiant whisper.

"I know you're there," Khan said, his voice trembling slightly. "Stop hiding. Show yourself."

Silence. Only the distant hum of the city and the wind whispering through the trees answered him. But he could feel him. Closer now.

A figure emerged from the shadows, a tall, slender man with eyes that seemed to absorb the moonlight. He smiled, a thin, cruel smile that sent a shiver down Khan's spine. He couldn't understand his face.

"You're very brave, Khan," he said, his voice smooth as silk. "But bravery can be foolish."

"Who are you?" Khan demanded, his voice stronger now.

"I am… a facilitator," he said, his smile widening. "A guide. A helper."

"You're a liar," Khan hissed. "You're manipulating everything."

He chuckled. "Manipulating? No, Khan. I'm simply… steering. Towards the inevitable."

"And what's inevitable?"

"The truth, of course." He stepped closer, his eyes glinting. "The truth about Mary. The truth about you. The truth about everything."

He reached out, Khan's fingers brushing his cheek. Khan flinched, but he didn't back away. He knew then that he couldn't run. He had to face him, face the truth, however painful it might be.

"Reivax gave me pieces," Khan said, "but you hold the full picture."

"Indeed," he said, "and I'm willing to share. But are you willing to see?"

He pulled a small, ornate box from his pocket. He opened it, revealing a single, tarnished silver locket.

"This belonged to Mary," Khan said. "It holds the key."

Khan reached for the locket, his fingers trembling. As he touched it, a wave of images flooded his mind, a kaleidoscope of memories, both his and Mary's. The truth, raw and unfiltered, crashed over him, a tidal wave of revelation.

She saw Mary's fear, her desperation, her final act of sacrifice. She saw the helper's role, his insidious influence, his manipulation of Mary's life.

The locket fell from his grasp, clattering on the pavement. Khan sank to her knees, the weight of the truth crushing him.

The helper knelt beside him, his voice soft, almost gentle. "Now you see, Khan. Now you understand."

Khan looked up at him, her eyes filled with tears. "Yes," he whispered, his voice hoarse. "I see."

Khan wanted to grasp the helper but vanished in thick air.

Khan wailed loudly.....

A phone call...Khan didn't pick up.

It rang again...Khan picked up.

Khan you should see this, I opened Sanvi's pillow,

What are you saying? How can you do that? Don't you remember the court order?

Khan listened to me, I remember the court order, I gave all the Pillows, but no one came for Sanvis yet, so I opened again, I opened it first but I didn't convey what I found earlier because you know, but this pillow is the college girl, Khan.

The killer is right under our nose, it is from the department... The Helper. The fingerprint matches.

Khan asked, with Whom? A scream heard from the other side.

Khan rushed towards Forensic… but it was late. Rekha was murdered.

Bad things are like unnoticed tears, it keeps on flowing until someone picks it up and heals.

~THE END~